'I'm not sure [what] to tell.'

Gaby threw him a quick glance. 'You know I'm a widow, that I have a son. You know I work for OBEX, that I'm a nurse, but that I am now employed as a counsellor. . .even if that is something you are not in favour of—'

'I also know you have red hair,' Armand interrupted softly, 'and very white skin that burns in the sun. . .'

Kids...one of life's joys, one of life's treasures.

Kisses...of warmth, kisses of passion, kisses from mothers and kisses from lovers.

In *Kids & Kisses*...every story has it all.

Laura MacDonald lives in the Isle of Wight. She is married and has a grown-up family. She has enjoyed writing fiction since she was a child, but for several years she worked for members of the medical profession, both in pharmacy and in general practice. Her daughter is a nurse and has helped with the research for Laura's medical stories.

Recent titles by the same author:

TOTAL RECALL
THE DECIDING FACTOR
IN AT THE DEEP END
STRICTLY PROFESSIONAL

FALSE PRETENCES

BY
LAURA MACDONALD

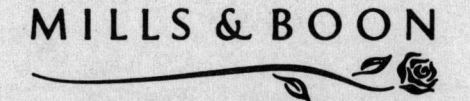

MILLS & BOON

DID YOU PURCHASE THIS BOOK WITHOUT A COVER?
If you did, you should be aware it is **stolen property** as it was reported *unsold and destroyed* by a retailer. Neither the Author nor the publisher has received any payment for this book.

All the characters in this book have no existence outside the imagination of the author, and have no relation whatsoever to anyone bearing the same name or names. They are not even distantly inspired by any individual known or unknown to the author, and all the incidents are pure invention.

All rights reserved including the right of reproduction in whole or in part in any form. This edition is published by arrangement with Harlequin Enterprises II B.V. The text of this publication or any part thereof may not be reproduced or transmitted in any form or by any means, electronic or mechanical, including photocopying, recording, storage in an information retrieval system, or otherwise, without the written permission of the publisher.

This book is sold subject to the condition that it shall not, by way of trade or otherwise, be lent, resold, hired out or otherwise circulated without the prior consent of the publisher in any form of binding or cover other than that in which it is published and without a similar condition including this condition being imposed on the subsequent purchaser.

*MILLS & BOON, the Rose Device and
LOVE ON CALL are trademarks of the publisher.
Harlequin Mills & Boon Limited,
Eton House, 18-24 Paradise Road, Richmond, Surrey TW9 1SR*

© Laura MacDonald 1996

ISBN 0 263 79604 3

*Set in Times 10 on 10 pt. by
Rowland Phototypesetting Limited
Bury St Edmunds, Suffolk*

03-9606-56714

*Made and printed in Great Britain
Cover illustration by Stewart Lees*

CHAPTER ONE

'You're going to love it here—I know you are. Sun, cheap booze, a fantastic social life and a heaven-sent opportunity to make money—what more could we ask for?' Martin Jackson grinned at Gaby across the gingham tabletop of the street café. A few yards away the Toulouse traffic roared past on the wide, tree-lined boulevard.

'I'm sure you're right.' Taking a sip of her *café au lait*, Gaby smiled at her seven-year-old son Oliver as he peered into a glass of orange juice and sucked up the contents through a multi-coloured straw. 'We like what we've seen so far, don't we, Oliver?'

The boy nodded without looking up, the sun catching the tips of his dark eyelashes and turning them the same burnished gold as his hair.

'So you're quite comfortable at Penny and Tom's?' Martin took a long draught of his beer, let out a deep sigh of contentment and leaned back in his chair, stretching out his legs in front of him.

Gaby nodded. 'I don't see how anyone could fail to be comfortable there—Penny's a dear and it's such a beautiful house.'

'Just an example of what can be achieved,' replied Martin. 'It was practically a ruin when they took it over and look at it now—one of the most prestigious properties in St Michel. You just have to make sure you approach the right people. . .'

'I dare say Tom's salary had something to do with it,' Gaby observed mildly. 'He's senior management now.'

Martin shrugged. 'I'm in line for promotion. . .' he trailed off, leaving the sentence unfinished, but his tone implied that anything Tom Shackleton had done he could do too. 'I've been at OBEX a long time,' he went on after a moment, justifying his position, 'neither did I make any bones about being transferred down here. Just give me a bit of time and I can achieve what Tom Shackleton has. I've told you before—I'd love to buy an old property and renovate it. We could have a place every bit as good as theirs—just you wait and see.'

'What's the factory like?' Deliberately changing the subject, Gaby threw Oliver an apprehensive look.

'No different from any other aircraft factory.' Martin shrugged, then, catching sight of her expression, he said, 'Honestly, Gaby, I swear when you're at work you'll think you're still at the Branchester plant.'

'If you say so.' She gave a faint smile. 'Although I've got a feeling I'm going to have to brush up on my French a lot more than you led me to believe. Penny and Tom speak excellent French.'

'They've been here a long time. . .'

'Harry's good at French,' observed Oliver suddenly, without looking up from his glass. 'He's going to teach me, he said. . .before I start school.'

'So you've made friends with young Harry Shackleton, then?' Martin turned to Oliver, who nodded in reply then noisily sucked up the last of his juice, earning a reproving look from Gaby.

Martin laughed. 'Told you he'd make friends, didn't I?' he teased. Leaning forward, he touched a strand of Gaby's deep auburn hair that had strayed from under her straw sunhat and now lay damply against her neck. Taking it between finger and thumb, he flicked it back over her shoulder. The gesture was both possessive and intimate, and once again Gaby found her gaze instinctively drifting to her son.

Oliver didn't seem to have noticed anything untoward, however, for as he wiped his mouth with the back of his hand he said, 'I still miss Matthew. . .'

'You're bound to miss your old pals for a while,' said Martin, 'but you'll soon settle down.'

'And Grandma,' said Oliver. 'I miss Grandma. . .'

'Of course you do,' murmured Gaby quickly, noticing the sudden brightness of her son's eyes. 'And Grandma will be missing you—which is why I think we should look for a card to send her.' Finishing her drink, she stood up. 'Is there somewhere we can buy cards, Martin?'

'Eh?' He looked up, apparently taken aback by the sudden change in conversation.

'Cards,' repeated Gaby patiently. 'Postcards of Toulouse that Oliver can send home.'

'Oh, right.' Martin drained his glass, then he too stood up, picking up car keys and sunglasses from the table. 'We'll go across to Le Capitol.'

Leaving the café, they crossed the road, Martin guiding them through the traffic then across an open-air street market selling everything from livestock and clothing to leatherware and household goods. Gaby would have liked to linger, but Martin forged ahead and she and Oliver were almost forced to run to keep up with him. They followed him into a covered mall of restaurants and shops packed with people, mostly students who sat at the tables talking and laughing. Someone was strumming a guitar, and at the end of the mall a colourful group of street players were performing a medieval pageant.

'You should be able to get what you want in any of these shops,' said Martin. 'They all sell souvenirs and cards.'

Oliver chose two cards—one of the Cathedral of Saint Étienne and one of Toulouse by night—and Gaby bought a poster of a Monet print. When they came out of the shops into the sunshine again Gaby was on the point of calling out to Martin, who was slightly ahead, to ask if they had time to go back to the street market, when suddenly Oliver began to cough.

Gaby threw him an anxious glance then, when the coughing continued, she stopped and, opening her shoulder bag, rummaged about inside. 'Come on, Oliver,' she said taking out an inhaler, shaking it and handing it to him, 'Use this.'

'Is he all right?' asked Martin, who had stopped to wait then walked back.

'He should be. The salbutamol usually acts fairly quickly,' said Gaby, watching Oliver closely as he used the inhaler. 'Is there somewhere we can sit down?' she asked after a moment.

Martin looked round. 'Over there.' He nodded across the road towards a large church surrounded by a paved area and shaded from the hot sun by a circle of plane trees.

Bench seats had been placed at intervals around the pink-bricked walls of the massive building, and as Gaby thankfully sat down, drawing Oliver down beside her, half a dozen well-fed pigeons waddled over to see what they had to offer.

'I thought you said his asthma had been OK since you arrived in France,' Martin observed, when Oliver's wheezing showed little signs of abating.

'It has,' said Gaby. 'Maybe it's the pollution from all this traffic—he's been fine in St Michel.'

They sat quietly for fifteen minutes, but Oliver showed no signs of recovery. 'He's only been this bad once before,' said Gaby, trying desperately to keep the anxiety from her voice, knowing the adverse effect it could have on Oliver.

'What do you want to do?' asked Martin after a further five minutes. Gaby thought she detected a note of impatience in his voice. 'Do you want to get him back to Penny's?'

'Last time he was this bad he needed to go on a nebuliser,' she murmured.

'Are you saying he needs a doctor?' By this time even Martin was beginning to look anxious.

Gaby nodded. 'But where. . .?'

Martin stood up, looked around, then craned his neck as if trying to get his bearings. 'I think,' he said, 'we are quite close to Dr Laurent's surgery.'

'Dr Laurent?' Gaby looked up hopefully. 'You mean—?'

'Yes, the factory doctor,' Martin answered, before she had time to finish the question. 'He lives here in town,' he said. 'In fact—yes, I'm right—it is quite near here. Look, if we go down that road there—' he nodded across the square '—we can cut through the back streets. . . Come on, I'll carry Oliver.' Bending down, he scooped up the boy from the seat and, carrying him in his arms like a baby, set off across the paving stones at a cracking pace, scattering the pigeons and leaving Gaby to keep up as best she could.

Somehow she managed to stay close, in spite of stumbling twice on the cobbles as they sped down back streets, away from the main boulevards, and into the very heart of the old city.

The streets were so narrow that the old stone-faced buildings towering on either side almost touched overhead. Because it had turned midday, already the wooden shutters that flanked every window had been closed, protecting the rooms within from the heat of the sun. In the silence their footsteps echoed eerily.

Martin seemed to know where he was going, but when they turned into a narrow, dark alleyway and passed beneath a low archway, Gaby, by this time gasping for breath, thought he must have lost his way. She could hardly imagine a doctor holding his surgery here, but even as the thought crossed her mind she caught the dim sheen of a brass plaque set into the wall.

A moment later, as Martin gave a grunt of satisfaction, the darkness suddenly gave way to startling, bright sunlight, and the alleyway opened out into a courtyard. On three sides, dark wooden balconies deep with shadows glowed with red geraniums, while in the far corner a narrow, rounded tower soared into the sky.

In spite of the urgency of the moment, Gaby paused, taken aback by the brightness, the colour and the stillness in this totally unexpected, almost secret place.

'Pull the bell!' Martin jerked his head towards a bell-pull beside a dark green door to one side of the tower. By this time he too was out of breath from the exertion of carrying Oliver, his face was red from the heat and he leaned against the wall to recover.

Gaby pulled the cord, and the clanging of the bell broke the silence. For several agonising moments Gaby thought there was no one at home. She turned from the door, her gaze flying from the two cars parked beneath the tower to Oliver, who had his eyes closed now, his head resting against Martin's chest.

'There's no one in, Martin. . .' Gaby began frantically, then, turning back, she gasped as she realised that the green door had noiselessly swung open and a tall, thin middle-aged woman was standing there, surveying them through a pair of tinted spectacles.

'Oh please, please can you help us?' asked Gaby, when it became apparent that the woman was waiting for her to speak. 'My son is having a severe asthma attack. . .is the doctor in?'

The woman's gaze flickered from Gaby to Martin and Oliver, then back to Gaby. Then she spoke in rapid French, much too fast for Gaby to follow.

Helplessly Gaby turned to Martin, who looked as if he too was struggling to understand.

'*Anglais*,' he said. 'Dr Laurent. . . OBEX doctor.'

The woman's expression changed. 'Voila! OBEX.' She nodded, standing aside for them to enter the building.

'Thank God!' Gaby muttered, and as Martin staggered forward with Oliver she followed behind.

It was cool and dim inside the house, behind the shutters. The woman motioned for them to wait, then turned and walked in an unhurried fashion towards a staircase in one corner of the vast hallway.

Gaby watched her go in an agony of anticipation, longing to intervene, to ask her to hurry, to say that the longer it took to get Oliver the much needed nebuliser the longer it would take for him to recover. But some sixth sense warned her that any attempt would be futile. This woman was not one to be hurried. Sedately, her back rigid, she mounted the staircase and walked round a gallery at the top, before knocking a closed door then disappearing inside.

'My back's killing me.' Still holding Oliver, Martin sank down with a groan onto an antique bench that ran almost the length of one wall, its seat and back padded with crimson brocade.

Gaby knelt on the floor beside them, and as she smoothed the damp hair from Oliver's forehead he opened his eyes and stared at her.

'It's all right, darling,' she whispered reassuringly, 'you'll be just fine.'

He continued to stare at her, his eyes enormous, his gaze solemn, unblinking, his breathing laboured, then, as she took one of his hands and gently chafed it between her own, his eyelids dropped again.

'Oh, come on!' Gaby looked round in growing desperation, her own nursing training unhelpful in her personal need. 'Is this his surgery or just where he lives?' she muttered, her gaze drifting from the polished wooden floor with its oriental rugs to the pieces of solid, dark antique furniture in the square-shaped hallway.

'Both, I think,' replied Martin abruptly. 'Don't really know much about him except that he comes into the factory a few times a week—nice enough chap, I believe, according to the men. . .'

'I don't really care what he's like, as long as he has a nebuliser for Oliver,' replied Gaby tightly.

'What if he hasn't?' Martin frowned.

'We get him to a hospital.'

'Right.'

They fell silent after that, and as Gaby's mind raced ahead, trying to cope with the possibility of an alternative course of action, she found herself watching particles of dust dancing in the shafts of sunlight that filtered through the closed shutters onto the polished floor.

She was just on the point of doing something—perhaps running up the stairs herself and hammering on the closed door at the end of the gallery—when the door opened and they heard the sound of voices. Scrambling to her feet, Gaby stood looking expectantly up the stairs, then the same woman appeared again and, leaning over the gallery rail, beckoned for them to come up.

Martin took a deep breath, visibly bracing himself, then stood up, and together the three of them made their way up the stairs.

The woman was waiting for them, and as they

reached the top she indicated for them to enter the room at the end of the gallery.

Sunlight spilled through the open door, and as they approached Gaby heard the rustle of a skirt, a ripple of laughter, but when they entered the room whoever had been there had disappeared through a door on the far side.

After the cool dimness of the rest of the house the brightness in the room was startling, and Gaby found herself wondering why the shutters hadn't been closed here also.

The thought was lost as her attention was taken by the man who turned from the window to face them. A man who was perhaps thirty-five, of slim build, with short, straight, dark hair, an olive complexion and dark, expressive eyes.

His gaze was calm, level as he stared at them—at her first, then Martin and Oliver, then back to her again before addressing Martin.

'It is Monsieur Jackson, isn't it?' he asked

Martin nodded. 'That's right.' He sounded vaguely surprised that the doctor should have remembered him. 'Can you see this little guy, Doc?'

'Put him over there.' The doctor pointed to a leather couch on the far side of the room, and for the first time Gaby realised that the room was a consulting room. As Martin placed Oliver onto the couch she too crossed the room and stood beside her son.

'Asthma, is it?' Reaching up, Dr Laurent pulled a blind down over the window, partly blocking the bright sunlight, before turning back to the couch.

'Yes.' Gaby gulped. 'He's had asthma for about three years now. It's been fairly well controlled. . . but this time. . .this time it hasn't responded to his salbutamol. . .' She trailed off as the doctor bent over Oliver. 'Do you have a nebuliser here, Doctor?'

In the space of time that it took for him to answer her question, Gaby suddenly, irrelevantly, became aware that a strong perfume lingered in the air—a distinctly feminine perfume that could only have belonged to the woman who had left the room as they had entered.

'Yes, I do have a nebuliser.' Dr Laurent turned to look at her, then, straightening up, he moved to a cupboard and, opening the doors, revealed shelves full of medical equipment and supplies.

At that moment Oliver suddenly became agitated, and while Gaby attempted to calm him Dr Laurent took a nebuliser from the cupboard, set it up on a small trolley beside the couch and placed the mask over the boy's nose and mouth.

As Oliver breathed in the fine spray produced by the nebuliser, and began to respond to the treatment, the tension in the room gradually eased.

Martin flopped down onto a hard-backed chair, and, producing a handkerchief from the pocket of his shorts, began to wipe the sweat from his forehead.

Dr Laurent moved away from the couch to a large desk beneath the window and began writing something on a pad, and Gaby drew a stool towards the couch, eased herself onto it and sat there, close to her son, gently stroking his hand.

The only sounds in the room were the ticking of a casement clock on the wall above the couch and Oliver's breathing.

It was Martin who spoke first. 'Will he need to go to hospital, Doc?' he asked, looking up suddenly.

'I do not think that will be necessary.' The doctor's English, although accented, was precise and beautifully modulated. 'The boy is responding well,' he went on, 'and I can loan you the nebuliser if necessary.'

'That's kind of you. Thank you.' Gaby threw him a grateful look, amazed that a stranger, even if he was a doctor, could be so considerate. Then she remembered that he wasn't exactly a stranger to Martin.

Martin stood up. 'I'd better go and get the car,' he said.

'Where is your car?' Dr Laurent looked up from the desk.

'In the big car park,' said Martin. 'The underground

one near the cathedral. I won't be long, Gaby.'

'No need for too much hurry, Monsieur Jackson,' said Dr Laurent. 'I want the boy to remain here for a while yet.'

'How long?' Martin looked at his watch.

The doctor shrugged, the gesture implying that they would be there just as long as it took for Oliver to recover. Without another word Martin left the room, and as the door closed behind him Dr Laurent said, 'Is there a problem? Some hurry?'

'Not really.' Gaby shook her head. 'At least, I don't think so. Martin has a day off from the factory. He was showing us the sights in Toulouse.'

'Ah, you like my city?' Dr Laurent looked up.

'Very much.' Gaby smiled at his sudden enthusiasm. It was as if it was important that she should like his city. 'At least,' she added, 'what I've seen of it so far.'

'You have come here to live?' He walked round the desk again, and for the first time Gaby noticed he was wearing a black polo-necked shirt, beautifully cut stone-coloured trousers and a narrow leather belt.

'Yes.' She nodded, paused, then added, 'For the time being anyway. If things work out.' She shrugged. 'Maybe it will be more permanent...I must say it's hot, though...far hotter than I thought it would be.'

'Yes,' he agreed, 'it has been very hot recently. You like the heat?' he added, eyeing the long turquoise Indian cotton skirt she was wearing and the straw hat with the floppy brim that she had dropped on the floor when they had first come into the room.

'I do like the sunshine,' she admitted. 'But I have to be careful, with my colouring, otherwise I burn.'

'Ah.' He smiled. 'The price one has to pay for Titian hair and skin like alabaster.'

She knew he was paying her a compliment, but a sudden wave of confusion left her incapable of receiving it graciously. Instead she felt an unbecoming flush touch the cheeks he had just likened to alabaster, and she lowered her gaze in embarrassment.

Apparently unperturbed, Dr Laurent moved to Oliver's side again to check his progress. 'He is doing well,' he said after a moment. 'You say he has had asthma for three years?'

'Yes.' Gaby nodded. 'I had hoped the climate here would help him. He's been fine in St Michel—that's where we are staying. This has only come on today—since we came into Toulouse.'

'There is much. . .petrol fumes. . .' Dr Laurent raised his hands, as if struggling to find the right word 'Pollution?' he asked, and when Gaby nodded, he went on, 'Yes, here in the city. But St Michel. . . St Michel, it is a small town. . .is countryside. . .much better for the boy.' He paused and looked down at Oliver. 'How old is he?'

'Seven,' Gaby replied.

'And he likes St Michel?'

'Oh, yes. . .he's made friends already, with the children of the family we are staying with. Oh, I expect you know them—Martin says you are the OBEX doctor.' He inclined his head slightly, in acknowledgement of the fact, and Gaby carried on, 'The Shackleton family. . . Tom and Penny?'

'Ah, yes.' He smiled. 'They are nice people.' He paused. 'I must confess, I have not seen your husband very much, Madame Jackson, but that can only be good, because it means he is very healthy and does not need to consult the factory doctor.' He laughed, and Gaby stared at him.

'Martin isn't my husband,' she said quickly. 'My name isn't Jackson, it's Dexter—Gaby Dexter.' Impulsively she held out her hand, then, feeling foolish, immediately wished she hadn't. But there was only a second's hesitation on Dr Laurent's part before he took her proferred hand.

'I am sorry,' he said, 'you must forgive me. I thought. . .' His gaze flickered to Oliver, who had opened his eyes and was gazing solemnly up at them over the rim of the nebuliser mask.

'It's all right,' replied Gaby quickly, aware of the renewed interest in his expression while he continued to hold her hand. 'It's a natural enough mistake under the circumstances. I am a widow,' she went on. 'My husband, Oliver's father, died in an accident nearly four years ago.'

He continued to stare at her and to hold her hand in his. 'And Monsieur Jackson?' he asked softly.

'He. . .' She found herself lowering her gaze from the intensity of his stare. 'He. . . Martin is a friend. . .a good friend.'

'He is your. . .boyfriend?' he said softly.

She raised her eyes again, and for the first time noticed that his eyes, dark as they were, had flecks of green in them. At the same moment as she nodded in reply to his question he marginally relaxed his grip on her hand, and she was able to withdraw it from his grasp.

'Ah.' The single word was like a long drawn-out sigh, but it seemed to carry a wealth of speculation. The next moment Dr Laurent was businesslike again— bending over Oliver, checking his condition, then walking back to his desk and writing on the pad once more.

Gaby sat in silence, watching Oliver but only too aware of the presence of the man behind the desk— so aware that she was relieved when shortly afterwards Martin returned.

'The traffic was horrendous,' he grumbled as he shut the door behind him. Neither Gaby nor Dr Laurent commented, and he sat down on the same chair he had vacated earlier, then, glancing at Oliver, and almost, it seemed, as an afterthought, said, 'How's he doing?'

'Very well.' It was Dr Laurent who answered. 'He needs to take things quietly for the next few days, and I suggest you take the nebuliser with you in case you need to use it again. But you should be able to take him home very shortly.'

'That's good.' Martin looked at his watch. 'Drinks at Mélisande Legrande's place tonight,' he said, then added, 'Wouldn't want to miss that.'

While Gaby remained silent, doubtful that she would be going anywhere else that day, Dr Laurent looked up from the desk.

Martin must have seen the doctor's apparent interest for he went on, 'Gaby hasn't met Mélisande yet, or

Julie Roberts and the rest of the gang, and, seeing she's going to be working with them, tonight has been especially arranged.'

'Working with them?' A frown creased Dr Laurent's forehead, and Gaby realised that he was staring at her in surprise.

'Yes.' Martin rushed on, not giving her a chance to reply for herself. 'Sorry, Doc, I should have said when we came in—but in all the fuss I didn't get round to it. Gaby is going to be working at OBEX, with the medical team. So I guess, in fact, that means you two will be working together.'

In the sudden silence Dr Laurent, ignoring Martin, continued to stare at Gaby. 'You are a nurse?' he asked quietly at last.

Gaby nodded. 'Yes, I am a nurse, but—'

'She's a counsellor,' Martin interrupted, giving her no time to explain.

'A counsellor?' Dr Laurent raised his eyebrows.

'Yes.' Gaby nodded again, poised to defend her corner, mindful of previous reactions from practitioners when they learned of her role. 'I was employed by OBEX as a counsellor at the Branchester factory. It was a new position, created to help staff cope with stress-related problems.' She paused. 'It proved to be such a success that management decided to introduce the scheme here at the Toulouse branch and appoint a counsellor.'

'I am aware of the management's decision,' Dr Laurent replied smoothly. 'I was consulted as to my opinion about such an appointment.'

'Oh, really?' Gaby began to relax. If he had sanctioned her position, her job would be all that much easier. 'Statistics in Branchester,' she went on enthusiastically, 'showed that many working days were being lost due to problems relating to personal stress.' She paused. 'No doubt the same situation was beginning to arise here in Toulouse, and my appointment was felt necessary.'

'Maybe.' Dr Laurent shrugged. 'But you will be hard pushed to convince me of that.'

Gaby drew in her breath quickly and stared at him. 'What do you mean?' she said, wondering if she had misheard but at the same time afraid that she hadn't.

'What I say,' he replied smoothly. 'I will need convincing of the merits of so-called "stress counselling".'

'But you said they consulted you about my appointment.' Gaby frowned, aware that Martin was looking from her to Dr Laurent in a bemused fashion.

'That is true.' Dr Laurent nodded. 'They did.'

'Then. . .?'

'I opposed it,' he replied. 'So you see, Madame Dexter, it is as I said. You will need to work very hard to convince me of its merits.'

CHAPTER TWO

ON THE way out Gaby, slightly flustered, found herself pausing to read the brass plaque on the wall as Martin lifted Oliver into the rear seat of his car. Its lettering stated that Armand Laurent, generalist, held his surgery in the building.

Armand. So that was his name. Gaby climbed into the car beside her son.

'Well, that turned out OK, didn't it?' Martin called over his shoulder as moments later he eased the car cautiously through the narrow back streets.

'It was very good of him to see Oliver,' Gaby replied. 'He'd obviously long finished his surgery.'

'Ah, it's not what you know—it's who you know,' chuckled Martin. 'It was the magic word OBEX that did it. I imagine he draws quite a tidy little sum each month from the company for his medical services.'

'I would hope his compassion as a doctor comes into it somewhere,' Gaby observed.

'I shouldn't count on it.' Martin chuckled again. He was silent for a moment, concentrating on the traffic, then he said, 'He didn't seem too happy about your appointment.'

'I'm well used to that sort of reaction from GPs,' replied Gaby. 'They soon change their tune when they find out how we ease their workload.'

'So you don't think he's going to be a problem for you?'

'Of course not,' she replied swiftly. 'In fact, I thought he was quite charming, really.'

'A bit too charming, if you ask me,' Martin grunted. 'Too smooth for my liking, some of these French guys,' he added after a moment.

It was on the tip of Gaby's tongue to ask him why he was planning to settle in their country if he felt that way, but she resisted the impulse, staring instead at the back of Martin's head. His fair hair curled into the back of his neck in exactly the same way as Terry's had. In fact, she could almost believe that it was Terry sitting there in the driving seat, that miraculously he had somehow been restored to her and Oliver.

She bit her lip and looked out of the window as Martin edged the car through the narrow back streets. She knew that she must try and stop thinking about Terry. He wasn't coming back, ever. She had to get used to that fact and get on with the rest of her life.

It wasn't as if she hadn't tried. Heaven knew how she'd tried. Since Terry's death she and Oliver had been living with her widowed mother, Lois, in their hometown of Branchester, and a year previously, in a desperate attempt to reassert herself, Gaby had taken the job with the medical team at the OBEX Aircraft Corporation. It was there that she'd met Martin Jackson, an aircraft design engineer, and had immediately been attracted by his resemblance to Terry.

She and Martin had gone out together for a few months, then Martin had been offered a post at the Toulouse factory. Gaby had thought that that would be the end of their relationship, then, quite by chance, she had heard that the company were to appoint a stress counsellor at the Toulouse factory for the British employees and their families.

'Why don't you apply for it?' Martin had said to her in a telephone conversation.

'I don't think so.' Her reply had been doubtful. 'I'm not sure it would be right for me—and besides, I have Oliver to consider.'

That might have been the end of the matter, but the following week Gaby's mother Lois had announced her engagement to an old friend of the family, and Gaby had found herself reassessing her own position.

On an impulse she'd applied for the job, not really thinking she stood a chance of getting it.

When the letter had arrived, saying that she had been successful, she had hardly been able to believe it.

'But where will we live?' she'd asked Martin on the phone.

'Penny Shackelton has said you can stay with them until you find something more permanent,' he replied. 'You remember Penny?'

'Yes,' she said faintly, 'I met her several times when her husband was at Branchester; she's a lovely person... But...I'm not sure, Martin.'

'Look,' he said, 'what I want to do is what some of the other guys have done—buy a dilapidated property and renovate it. I know it'll take some time, but by then—who knows?—maybe you'll be ready to move in with me.'

'I don't know, Martin...I'm really not sure about that,' she said cautiously.

'OK, I'm not trying to rush you. If it works out, fine. If it doesn't, well...at least you will have tried.'

And she still wasn't sure now, she thought as she stared at the back of Martin's head. She'd voiced the same fears to her mother, and her reply had been similar to Martin's.

'You'll never know, darling, if you don't give it a try.'

'But suppose none of it works out—suppose I'm making a big mistake?'

'In that case you come back here.'

'But what about Oliver?' she'd said. 'Is it fair to keep uprooting him like that?'

'The experience will be good for him,' Lois had said firmly. 'He'll learn to speak French; he'll make new friends. And France isn't exactly the ends of the earth, for heaven's sake... Besides, the climate down there in the south might be better for his asthma.'

And it had been—until today, Gaby thought as Martin took the wide autoroute out of the city.

On one side they passed the large, modern airport terminal and the huge OBEX factory complex, while on the other the river, glittering in the afternoon sunshine, snaked its way beneath a series of bridges against the backdrop of Toulouse—La Ville Rose—so aptly named for its pink-bricked buildings.

Maybe Dr Laurent had been right, and Oliver's attack had simply been a result of the inevitable pollution in the city. Dr Laurent. Gaby's thoughts lingered for a moment on the man who had been so kind to Oliver, the man with whom in the future she would be working. The man who had made it quite plain that he was not in favour of stress counselling.

There had been something unusual about him, something Gaby wasn't quite able to put her finger on. He had seemed very different from the men she usually met—the men at the factory, the men at home in Branchester. 'Smooth', Martin had called him, but that wasn't it—it was more than that—much more than that.

There had been some quality about the whole episode that Gaby was quite at a loss to define—the stillness of the unexpected sun-filled courtyard in the heart of the city, the geranium-filled balconies, the tower in the corner like something out of Grimms' fairy tales, and, inside, the cool, dim hallway, the sun-filled room, the forgotten shutters. There had been someone with him seconds before they had entered that room, they had heard her laughter. . .his wife, maybe?

'Are you asleep in the back? Am I talking to myself?'

With a guilty start Gaby realised that Martin had been talking, and because she had become so lost in her thoughts she hadn't heard a word he'd been saying.

'I'm sorry, Martin,' she replied, with a swift glance at Oliver revealing that he appeared to be asleep. 'What were you saying?'

'Only that I'll drop you off at Tom's then go back to my lodgings and shower and change. We don't need to be at Mélisande's until six, but the traffic could be heavy, so we'd best leave about five-thirty.'

Gaby took a deep breath. 'I'm sorry, Martin,' she said, 'you're going to have to go without me.'

'What d'you mean?' He half turned his head, enough for Gaby to see the frown that creased his forehead.

'I can't leave Oliver tonight,' she said quietly.

'Surely he'll be OK now?' There was a note of

exasperation in Martin's voice. 'Besides, Mélisande has arranged this drinks party especially so that you can meet the others.'

'I know that, and I can only hope she will understand,' replied Gaby patiently, sensing a battle. 'But I couldn't possibly leave Oliver. He may have another attack.'

'The girl who helps the Shackletons. . .what's her name?' Martin called over his shoulder.

'Adèle.'

'Yes, Adèle. . .she seems a sensible enough sort of girl.'

'She is. But even so. . .'

'I'll be all right, Mum.' Gaby glanced down and saw that Oliver had opened his eyes and was gazing solemnly up at her. 'I don't mind if you go out.'

'There you are, you see.' Martin laughed. 'Worrying about nothing again.'

Gaby remained silent and stared out of the car window. They had left the city far behind and were travelling through an avenue of tall poplars fringing the road and forming the boundary for acres of fields and farming land.

There seemed to be very little traffic at that time of the afternoon, and when they finally entered the small town of St Michel it was to find it deserted. The central market square, like some vast arena, was empty after the morning's trading, and the shutters on the well-kept houses that surrounded the square were tightly closed against the blistering sun.

Not for the first time since arriving in France, Gaby wondered where everyone was. She knew that at the magic hour of four o'clock everything would come alive again—the shutters would be thrown open, the traffic would roll. . .but still she wondered just what went on behind those shutters each day.

The old farmhouse that Tom and Penny Shackleton had bought and renovated was in open countryside on the far side of St Michel. Set into a small, natural hillside, it was protected on three sides by clumps of poplars and tall cypress trees. Its walls were covered in creamy grey stucco and the roof was of warm ochre ridge tiles, while the inevitable shutters, tightly closed over each window, were painted a pale aquamarine blue.

The attic window high in the roof was crowned by a rounded gable, giving it the appearance of a tiny bell-tower, while the double-fronted doors, painted the same blue as the shutters, were surrounded by a creeping red-leafed ivy. Beneath every window shallow wooden boxes overflowed with busy Lizzie and pink and red geraniums.

When Martin drove into what had once been the old farmyard, and which was now a rather impressive forecourt, two collared doves, disturbed from their afternoon siesta, rose from the roof of an outhouse and, cooing in protest, fluttered down onto the flagstones. Penny's red saloon was parked at one side of the house and an ancient black bicycle, belonging to Adèle, was propped against the trunk of a plane tree.

Martin brought the car to a halt and switched off the engine, then, as he climbed out, Gaby also opened her door and stepped out onto the flagstones.

'I must get Oliver inside out of this heat,' she said.

'Shall I carry him?' asked Martin, but before Gaby had the chance to answer, Oliver opened his door and scrambled from the car.

'It's OK,' he said. 'I'm all right.' Without a backward glance he walked to the front doors, pushed them open and disappeared inside while Gaby and Martin stood and watched him.

'He seems fine now,' observed Martin.

Gaby nodded. 'I hope so.' Bending down, she retrieved her sunhat and the nebuliser from the car, then, straightening up, she turned to Martin again. 'Thanks for all your help today,' she said softly.

Martin shrugged, then, glancing at his watch, said, 'Well, I'd best be off. I'll be back at about five-thirty for you.'

Gaby had started to follow Oliver into the house, but she paused at Martin's words, then turned again and faced him. 'I won't be going to Mélisande's,' she said quietly, and as his expression changed to one of exasperation she went on, 'I thought I'd made that plain.'

'I don't understand why,' said Martin sharply.

'I told you. I need to stay with Oliver.'

'Oliver will be all right. Even he said so himself.'

'Oliver is a child,' Gaby retorted, stung suddenly by Martin's apparent lack of understanding, 'a very young child. Besides, it's not for him to make that sort of decision.'

'You're being over-protective,' said Martin tightly.

'Maybe. Maybe not.' Gaby shrugged but, remaining unmoved, added, 'He could quite easily have another attack, and if he does I intend to be on hand.'

'For goodness' sake, Gaby.' Martin stared at her, his hands on his hips. 'Oliver could have an asthma attack at any time—do you intend being "on hand", as you put it, for the rest of his life?'

'I'm sorry, Martin—I'm not going to argue with you,' Gaby replied. 'It's what I've decided, and that's that.' She turned again, but once more Martin intervened.

'And what am I supposed to tell Mélisande, after all the trouble she's gone to to arrange this evening for your benefit?' he demanded.

'Tell her I'm sorry,' Gaby replied, then added, 'Or, if you prefer, I'll phone and tell her myself.' She paused, and when he didn't reply she went on, 'As for the evening being arranged purely for me. . .I appreciate the intention, but I rather suspect there would have been a party of some description anyway. From what I've seen so far an excuse isn't really needed.'

Martin stopped scowling. 'I told you the social life was good, didn't I?'

'Yes, Martin, you certainly did. Now—' her tone softened '—I really must go and see to Oliver. . .'

'OK.' He sighed, but sounded resigned. 'I'll see you tomorrow after work—don't forget it's Charles and Lisa's barbecue.' With a wave of his hand he got into the car, started the engine, reversed, then roared out of the yard in a cloud of dust.

Gaby watched him go, then, with a sigh, turned and wearily entered the house.

It was dim in the hall after the glare outside, and cool due to the two fans that whirred softly overhead. There was no sign of Penny or Adèle, so Gaby made her way upstairs to the two small bedrooms at the top of the house that had been allocated to Oliver and herself. She found Oliver sitting on the side of his bed and, sinking down beside him, she took his hand.

'How are you feeling?' she asked.

'Not too bad. Are you going out?' The question was casual, but Gaby detected a trace of anxiety behind it.

'No,' she replied firmly. 'Not tonight, nor any night until you are completely better.'

'I 'spect I would be all right with Adèle,' he said dubiously.

'Ah, but would Adèle be all right with you?' Gaby smiled and ruffled his hair. 'It wouldn't be fair on her, would it? She's not used to dealing with asthma attacks.'

'Nor is Martin, is he?' said Oliver solemnly.

'No, darling, he isn't,' replied Gaby. 'But he was very good to you today, getting you to the doctor.'

'He was nice—that doctor,' said Oliver thoughtfully. 'I liked him. Do you think we'll see him again?'

'Well, I certainly shall, because Dr Laurent is the factory doctor, and when I start work next week I shall be working with him.' Gaby glanced up as there came a sound outside in the passage, then Penny suddenly appeared in the open doorway.

'Oh, you *are* back,' she said. 'I thought I heard voices.' Penny looked hot; her long dark hair was drawn back from her face and secured with a band. She looked curiously from one to the other. 'Is everything all right?' she asked, as if sensing that something had happened.

'Oliver had a bad asthma attack while we were in Toulouse,' explained Gaby.

'Oh, I say. Poor old you.' Penny looked down at Oliver in concern. 'OK now?' Her glance darted questioningly to Gaby.

'Yes, we think so—with a little help from that.' Gaby nodded towards the nebuliser that she'd placed on the bed.

'Whatever is it?' Penny frowned.

'A nebuliser,' explained Oliver. 'It helps me breathe, doesn't it, Mum?' When Gaby smiled in agreement, he went on, 'The doctor let us bring it home.'

'Doctor?' Penny raised her eyebrows in surprise. 'You had to see a doctor?'

'Yes. Oliver's inhaler wasn't having any effect, so Martin took us to see a Dr Laurent. The factory doctor.'

'Oh, Armand?' said Penny.

'You know him?' Gaby looked up quickly.

'Yes. At least, not that well,' Penny corrected herself. 'He came to see Charlotte when she had a very high temperature once, and I've met him a couple of times at functions—that's all.'

'So are you registered with him because he is the factory doctor?'

'Not exactly,' replied Penny. 'It doesn't quite work that way here. Patients aren't registered with a specific doctor—they keep their own records and can consult which doctor they please. But I suppose you could say we consulted Armand Laurent because he is the factory doctor. . .it just made sense, really. . .' She trailed off. 'What did you think of him?' she added.

'He was nice.' It was Oliver who answered. 'I liked him.'

'Yes,' Gaby agreed, 'he was. Now, Oliver—' she turned to her son '—I want you to rest.'

'I'll get Adèle to bring his tea up,' said Penny, and turned to leave the room. As she reached the door she paused and looked back. 'What are you going to do about Mélisande's party?' she asked.

'I won't be going,' replied Gaby firmly, then, seeing Penny's expression, said quickly, 'I don't want to leave Oliver.'

'I'm sure Adèle would—' Penny began, but Gaby cut her short.

'I'm sure she would too, but it wouldn't be fair—to either of them,' she added.

'Martin was cross,' said Oliver suddenly.

'Was he?' Penny looked quickly at Gaby.

'He said the party was for Mum. I said she could go. . .'

'If it would help. . .' Penny hesitated. 'I'll stay with Oliver.'

'That's kind of you, Penny.' Gaby stood up. 'But I'm not going anywhere. I'm sure this Mélisande Legrand will understand when she knows the circumstances, and if she doesn't—well, there's nothing I can do about it. My place is with my son when he is ill.'

'And Martin?' Penny raised her eyebrows.

'He'll have to get used to the idea as well,' retorted Gaby.

Later, when Oliver was resting, Gaby went down to the kitchen to get herself a drink. She found Penny ironing a pair of trousers.

'Is Oliver all right?' Penny looked up as Gaby took a carton of orange juice from the fridge.

'Yes, I think so.' Gaby sighed. 'His breathing is still a bit wheezy. I shall keep an eye on him and put him on the nebuliser again if necessary.'

'I meant what I said about looking after him, if you really want to go tonight.'

'Yes, I know you did, Penny,' Gaby replied, 'and I really appreciate it. But I wouldn't enjoy myself if I did go, so there isn't really a lot of point. Besides, it would be a shame for you to miss it.'

'Yes, a great shame.' Penny pulled a face.

'Do I detect a certain reluctance on your part?' asked Gaby curiously.

With a sigh, Penny stood the iron on end. 'Not really. Although, if I'm honest, I do get a bit fed up with all this socialising. Oh, don't get me wrong,' she said, seeing Gaby's slightly surprised expression, 'I know it's important to Tom, and his position in management requires it and all that, but it all gets a bit of a bind at times... It was great when we first came out here—in fact, I thought it was wonderful, all the parties and barbecues and things—but just lately...oh, I don't know...'

She trailed off, then held up the beige silk trousers she had been ironing. 'I hope these will be all right to wear tonight—that's if I can get into them. I seem to be waging a constant battle with my weight since Sam was born...' she trailed off again, then after a moment said, 'No doubt Mélisande Legrande will be wearing some chic little number, as usual... Have you met her yet, Gaby?'

'Mélisande?' Gaby sipped her orange juice. 'No...but I gather from Martin she's the secretary who does all the work for the medical team, so I shall be working with her.'

'Hmm, she's also Tom's secretary,' replied Penny stiffly.

Gaby looked up sharply, but Penny had leaned over by then to unplug the iron and Gaby couldn't see her expression. By the time Penny straightened up, the moment had passed.

'Martin said something about a barbecue tomorrow night,' Gaby remarked as she watched Penny return the ironing board to its cupboard.

'Oh, Lord, yes. I'd forgotten that.' Penny rolled her eyes. 'Still, that shouldn't be too bad—and at least we can take the kids. It's these dreadful, standing around drinks parties that bore me to tears.'

Gaby smiled, and although she felt inclined to agree with Penny she refrained from doing so. It was far too soon for her to be voicing controversial opinions. Instead, as Penny disappeared upstairs, muttering something about finding a suitable top to wear with her trousers, Gaby followed her, slowly making her way back to Oliver's room.

For the next hour or so she read to Oliver from his favourite Roald Dahl book. Later they heard sounds outside, and when Gaby looked out of the window she was in time to see Penny and Tom getting into Tom's pale blue Renault. Penny was wearing a black pleated blouse with her beige trousers, and Tom looked handsome in casual evening wear. He glanced up, and, catching sight of Gaby at the window, waved to her before he closed his car door.

She waved back, not in the least envious that she was unable to go with them, then, as the sound of their car faded into the distance, the bedroom door was cautiously pushed open and Harry's tousled head appeared.

'Can I come and listen?' he asked Gaby, at the same time suspiciously eyeing Oliver.

'Course you can.' Gaby made space for him on the bed.

'Is he ill?' Still Harry eyed his friend.

'He has been,' replied Gaby. 'But don't worry, you won't catch anything.' As she spoke there came a scuffle from outside the door, and first five-year-old Sam, then, more slowly, Charlotte appeared, desperately trying to be sophisticated but equally enthusiastic.

'Can we come as well?' asked Sam, his eyes like saucers.

Gaby laughed, and made even more room on the bed.

'Are you sure we won't catch anything?' Charlotte looked wary. 'When my friend had measles, Mummy said not to go and see her.'

'Oliver has asthma, not measles,' said Gaby. 'Asthma is a condition, not a disease.'

'What's a condition?' asked Harry.

'Well, it's something that happens in a person's body. In asthma it's a narrowing of the little tubes in someone's lungs,' explained Gaby patiently.

'Why?' asked Charlotte suspiciously.

'We're not really sure. Something must happen to trigger an attack, but in Oliver's case we're not absolutely sure what it is.'

'What sort of things?' Harry settled himself more comfortably on the bed.

'Sometimes it can be certain plants or animal fur that cause asthma,' explained Gaby, 'but in Oliver's case we think it might be something to do with the weather, or with the fumes from the traffic. It came on today when we were in Toulouse. Martin—Mr Jackson—took us to see Dr Laurent, and he let Oliver use that nebuliser.' Gaby pointed to the machine that she had placed on a chest of drawers.

'How does it work?' Harry slipped off the bed and went to study the nebuliser.

'You pour liquid into it,' said Gaby, 'and the patient puts the mask over his face and inhales the droplets from the liquid.'

'Did you have to do that?' Sam stared at Oliver in awe.

Oliver nodded importantly.

'Dr Laurent came to see me,' announced Charlotte, her tone indicating that she considered Oliver had had quite enough attention. 'I liked him—my friend Becky thinks he's dead dishy.'

'Does she, now?' Gaby raised an eyebrow in Charlotte's direction, at the same time trying to remember if she too had found men dishy at nine years old.

'Can we have the story now?' asked Harry, obviously bored with the whole asthma business.

Gaby smiled and turned back to the beginning of the book again, knowing that Oliver wouldn't mind how many times he heard it. She had only just started to read when there came a tap on the door and Adèle, the young French girl who helped Penny with the house and the children, popped her head round.

'Ah!' The worried expression in her large brown eyes cleared as she caught sight of the children. 'I wonder if they with you. You mind?' she asked Gaby.

'No, Adèle.' Gaby smiled. 'Of course I don't mind.'

Although Oliver's breathing continued to be rather wheezy, the night passed without him suffering another attack. Gaby left the communicating door open between their bedrooms, and when she awoke the following morning she could tell from the sound of his breathing that Oliver was still asleep.

She slipped out of bed, pulled a cotton wrap over

her nightdress, padded quietly to the door and stood for a moment watching her son. The gold hair, so like his father's, was damp, tousled and sticking out in spikes from his head. The thick gold-tipped eyelashes rested on his freckle-smattered cheeks and one arm was flung above his head.

Quietly, so as not to wake him, Gaby turned away, tiptoed to the window in her own room, unlatched it and pushed open the shutters. The bedroom, on the east side of the house, looked out over a field of scarlet poppies and beyond, over acres of surrounding farmland, full of ripening crops.

A light early mist lay over the fields, shrouding the sun, and as Gaby rested her elbows on the windowsill and breathed in the fresh morning air she heard the sound of a cuckoo from the thicket behind the house. She had heard the sound each morning since she and Oliver had arrived, and she still felt surprised and at the same time comforted at such an English sound so far south.

A movement caught her eye on the road beyond the poppyfield, a black speck in the distance which, as it drew nearer, Gaby realised was Adèle on her bicycle. The French girl, she knew, would have been on her usual early-morning trip into St Michel. Moments later Adèle left the road, bumping her bicycle up a grass track at the side of the house, then, dismounting, she walked the last few yards. Leaning out of the window, Gaby saw several loaves protruding from a basket on the bicycle handlebars, and at the same moment caught the unmistakable aroma of freshly baked bread.

'Mum, is it time to get up?' Oliver's voice came to her through the open bedroom door.

Gaby withdrew her head and closed the window.

Later, after she and Oliver had showered and dressed, they went downstairs to find that Tom had gone to work and Penny had already left to take the children to the convent school they attended on the far side of St Michel.

'She said to tell you she going on to shops in Toulouse,' said Adèle. 'She be back later.'

'Thanks, Adèle,' Gaby walked to the open kitchen door. 'I think we'll take our breakfast outside—it's not too hot yet.'

'I buy chocolate croissants for Oliver,' said Adèle, smiling.

'Brill—they're my favourite!' Oliver's eyes shone.

'You spoil him, Adèle,' said Gaby.

'He been ill. He need spoiling,' protested Adèle. 'He better today?' she added as an afterthought.

'Yes.' Gaby nodded. 'He's still wheezing a bit, but he's better than he was yesterday. I think, however, that he should take things very quietly today.'

'What is this "wheezing"?' Adèle looked mystified.

Gaby attempted to demonstrate with a wheezy-sounding cough.

They were all laughing when the kitchen phone suddenly rang, and Adèle turned and lifted the receiver. She spoke rapidly in French, paused, then looked at Gaby. '*Oui*—yes, yes. She here,' she said, then, passing the receiver to Gaby, she added, 'For you—Monsieur Jackson.'

'Oh.' The laughter stopped abruptly, and Gaby took the receiver. 'Hello, Martin?' she said.

'Gaby? How are things?'

'Oliver is quite a lot better this morning.'

'Good. You missed a great party last night.'

'Really?' She paused. 'I hope you gave my apologies to Mélisande.'

'What? Oh, yes, yes, I did.' He sounded vague, then quickly, before she could say more, went on, 'Guess what? Last night Charles told me about a property that is for sale. Apparently it's only the old shell of a farm cottage. . .but it's going for a song.'

'Won't it need a lot of money spending on it, if it's only a shell?' asked Gaby dubiously.

'Yes, but Charles says the French Government give substantial grants towards that sort of thing. . . Anyway, Charles is going to make some enquiries about it for me. But I must go now, Gaby, I'm supposed to be working. I'll see you tonight.'

'Tonight?' Her fingers tightened instinctively round the receiver.

'Yes, the barbecue. I'll pick you up around six.'

'But. . .' She was about to say that she would have to see how Oliver was by then, but Martin had hung up and the line had gone dead. She stared at the receiver for a moment, then with a little shrug she turned, only to find that Oliver and Adèle had gone outside.

She found them sitting at the large wooden table beneath a vine-covered loggia where the Shackleton family ate most of their meals. Oliver had started his croissants, and she saw that Adèle had carried out a tray filled with fresh coffee, the bread she had seen in the bicycle basket, some pats of butter and a pot of greengage jam.

'I leave you to it.' Adèle beamed as Gaby sat down beside Oliver. 'You enjoy breakfast.' She picked up the empty tray and made her way back into the house.

'Mum?' Oliver looked up, wiping flakes of croissant and smears of chocolate from his mouth. 'When will I go to school?'

'Next week,' she replied, pouring coffee into a blue and white china cup, 'when I start work.'

'Do you think I'll be in the same class as Harry?' Oliver sounded anxious.

'Yes, love, I'm sure you will.' Gaby hastened to reassure him, knowing that any form of stress was the last thing he needed. She watched him for a moment as he finished the last of his croissant, then, leaning back in her seat, she lifted her face to the sun and briefly closed her eyes. 'It's lovely here, isn't it?' she murmured after a moment. When Oliver didn't reply, she opened one eye and looked at him. 'You do like it here, don't you, Oliver?'

'S'all right.' His reply was non-committal. 'I like these croissants,' he added after a moment.

As Gaby hid a smile at his pronunciation of the word he said, 'Can I go and do those cards for Grandma and Matthew now?'

'Yes.' She nodded. In all the excitement she'd

forgotten the cards they'd bought in Toulouse. 'They're in my handbag in the bedroom.'

Oliver slipped from his chair, ran indoors, and only minutes later was back with the cards. Laboriously, with a black ballpoint pen, he wrote his messages, then Gaby helped him with the addresses.

Afterwards they both cleared the table, and while Gaby washed the breakfast china Oliver disappeared upstairs on some mission of his own. When she had tidied the kitchen Gaby felt restless, wanting to do something but not really knowing what. She could hear Adèle vacuuming upstairs, but the rest of the house was quiet.

In the end she wandered into the sitting room, chose a paperback book from the bookcase, then went back into the garden and sat beneath the loggia again.

She quickly became engrossed in the story, but as it grew warmer in the garden she found it more and more difficult to concentrate. She was vaguely aware of Oliver's voice as he chattered to Adèle, then, as if they had a will of their own, her eyelids began to droop.

She was awakened by a light touch on her arm. For one moment, as she struggled to recall where she was, she imagined it must be a fly or some other insect, then as it came again she opened her eyes fully and looked up.

A figure stood in front of her, blocking the light. For one moment she thought it was Adèle, but then, as her vision readjusted, to her amazement she found herself gazing up into the face of Armand Laurent.

CHAPTER THREE

'I AM sorry.' The voice was pleasant, accented, and so instantly recognisable that even if Gaby thought her eyes might have deceived her she was assured that her ears had not. 'I did not mean to startle you—I could not make anyone hear in the house.'

'Oh, they must be upstairs,' she replied stupidly. 'I was reading—I must have dropped off to sleep—it's so warm. . .I. . .we weren't expecting anyone. . .'

She trailed off in confusion.

'I am thinking it is a good thing I come.' He spoke solemnly, but Gaby thought she detected a glimmer of amusement in his dark eyes.

'You are. . .?'

'Yes, I fear if you had remained undisturbed your nose would have turned really red, then it would have blistered, and finally peeled. As it is, it is still only a delicate shade of pink.'

'Oh!' Gaby gasped and covered her nose with her hand. 'I've got sunblock on—I didn't think. . .'

'It is very hot.' He spread his hands. 'And you do not wear your hat today.'

'I forgot,' Gaby muttered. 'I must get it.' She struggled to get out of the chair, aware of how she must look in her baggy green T-shirt and white shorts, her face shiny, with no make-up, her hair screwed up into a topknot and, if all that wasn't enough, apparently with a red nose. As she struggled to her feet, however, she remembered her manners. 'Have you come to see Oliver?' she asked.

'Yes.' He smiled. 'I was in the area and thought I would call to see how he is today.'

'He's much better,' replied Gaby, making a determined effort to pull herself together.

'No more attacks?'

'No. His breathing has still been rather wheezy, but nothing like it was yesterday.'

'So you have not had to use the nebuliser again?'

She shook her head. 'Do you want to take it back? I'll get it for you. . .'

'No. I have not come for that,' he replied firmly. 'I would prefer you to keep it—at least for the time being. No, I come because I am concerned. When you were not at the party last evening, I thought—'

'You were at the party?' Her eyes widened in surprise.

'Yes.' He nodded.

She turned away, her mind racing. It hadn't for one moment occured to her that he might have been there, but, when she really thought about it, it wasn't so surprising. If what Martin had said was right, the party had apparently been arranged with her in mind; she was to work with the OBEX medical team, and Dr Laurent was the OBEX doctor.

'I think Mélisande thought it would be nice for us to meet before we actually start work,' he said, echoing her own thoughts.

For the first time Gaby felt a twinge of regret that she hadn't been able to go.

'I saw Monsieur Jackson there,' Dr Laurent went on, 'and he said you were staying with Oliver. I thought maybe the boy was worse.'

'No.' Gaby sighed. Did no one understand? 'Oliver was no worse. But there was always the chance he might be. I wouldn't have dreamt of leaving him under such circumstances. . .'

'I quite understand,' he replied quietly, but Gaby, irritated now by everyone's apparent insensitivity, swept on, ignoring him.

'I know everyone thought I was foolish, and I know that Adèle is quite competent, but. . .'

'I said I quite understand,' he repeated, and when she drew breath he added, 'You are his mother, he is seven years old, he is in a strange country amongst strangers, he was distressed. . .It is the most natural thing in the world that you should choose to stay with your son instead of attending a rather tedious drinks party.'

'Oh!' She stared at him in amazement as it gradually dawned on her that he was actually on her side.

'So, now that I am here,' he went on, his voice softening, 'I think I should at least see the boy.'

'What?' she stared at him, almost mesmerised by the expression in his dark eyes. 'Oh, yes, yes of course,' she mumbled at last. 'I'll go and fetch him—I think he must be upstairs.' With her head down, she brushed past him and stumbled into the house.

Only too aware that he was standing there beneath the loggia watching her, she called out to Oliver.

To her dismay there was no reply, either from Oliver or from Adèle, and a hurried search revealed that the house was empty. In the bedroom she allowed herself a surreptitious glance in the mirror, groaned at what she saw, dragged out the band securing her hair, and desperately, but without success, tried to tame the wild cloud.

In the end she was forced to return to the garden, where she found Dr Laurent leaning against the table and flicking through the pages of the paperback she had been reading. He glanced up as she approached.

'I can't seem to find Oliver for the moment,' she said quickly, not giving him the chance to speak first. 'He must be helping Adèle with something. . .'

'Please. . .do not worry.' He put the book back onto her chair. 'If that is the case, he must be better, and that is my only concern.'

'I'm sorry, Dr Laurent. . .and after you coming all this way.' Gaby lowered her gaze to hide her embarrassment.

'Please. . . Armand,' he said.

'I'm sorry?' Quickly she looked up again.

'My name is Armand,' he said.

'Oh, right.' She nodded, more uncomfortable than ever.

'We are to work together, to be colleagues. . .' He paused.

Desperately Gaby sought for something to say.

'Am I to call you Madame Dexter?' he asked softly at last.

'What?' She was startled for the moment, amazed that he should even think that would be the case—at the Branchester factory it was all Christian names amongst the staff—then once again she saw the glimmer of amusement in his eyes.

'So what is it to be?' He was smiling now, a quizzical smile. 'Madame Dexter?'

'Of course not,' she replied. 'My name's Gaby.'

He stared at her.

'Gaby,' she repeated. 'Gaby Dexter.'

When he still continued to stare, she frowned. 'What is it?' she asked. 'What's wrong?'

'Gaby?' He was frowning now. 'You say this before, at my house. But what is it, this Gaby?'

'What do you mean?' It was Gaby's turn to stare, and she was aware that she sounded indignant.

'This word. I never hear it before. It is—how you say?—a nickname? Yes, is that it? This Gaby?'

'Oh!' A smile touched her lips as she understood the reason for his bewilderment. 'No, it is not exactly a nickname, it's an abbreviation—my name is Gabrielle,' she explained, 'but everyone calls me Gaby. They always have done,' she added as he began to shake his head.

'But why?' He sounded genuinely perplexed. 'I don't understand.' He was staring intently at her now, and yet again she felt a wave of embarrassment.

'Well, you have to admit—' she gave a little shrug '—Gabrielle is a bit of a mouthful. . .'

'It is a beautiful name.'

'Yes, but. . .'

'It is sacrilege to mutilate it.'

'Oh, steady on—' she was laughing now '—that's a bit strong.'

'No, I mean it,' he said.

She stared at him, the smile fading from her lips as she realised that this time he really was serious. She was saved from finding anything else to say by the sound of voices drifting through the garden—Adèle's heavily accented English and Oliver's high-pitched chatter as they came round the side of the house.

'Mum!' Oliver's voice rose to a squeak of excitement. 'Adèle took me down to the stream. There are ducks down there—they've got babies. . .' He trailed off as he caught sight of the doctor.

'I shall call you Gabrielle.' Armand spoke so quietly that only she could have heard.

Hastily Gaby turned to her son. 'Oliver. . .' Her voice faltered slightly. 'Dr Laurent has called in to see how you are today.'

'I'm fine now, thank you.' Oliver looked from his mother to the doctor, then back to Gaby again. 'Aren't I, Mum?'

'Well, you certainly seem to be a lot better,' she replied.

'Harry said there's a barbecue this evening,' said Oliver quickly, as if he had suddenly seen a golden opportunity and didn't want to miss it. 'Can we go? Please? Mum?'

Gaby glanced at Armand. 'Maybe you should ask Dr Laurent,' she murmured.

Oliver looked at Armand again, and this time he appeared to be holding his breath. 'Can I?' he breathed.

'I do not see why not.' Armand smiled, and Adèle, who suddenly seemed quite overcome by the whole thing, breathed a sigh of relief and dissolved into a torrent of French.

Armand laughingly replied, and as Adèle hurried away into the house he turned to Gaby. 'She's gone to prepare coffee,' he explained simply.

'In that case, I suggest we sit down.' Gaby turned to the chair where she had been sitting earlier. 'But first, I think I'll move my chair into the shade.'

'A very good idea.' Armand laughed, and as Gaby picked up her chair and moved it to a far corner of the yard beneath the branches of a eucalyptus tree he picked up a second chair and joined her. Oliver, happy at the turn events seemed to be taking, ran into the house.

'You realise you've probably made Oliver's day by saying he can go to the barbecue,' said Gaby, then, on a sudden impulse, she added, 'Will you be going, Dr Laurent?'

'Armand,' he said seriously. 'Please. Armand.'

'Very well.' She took a deep breath. 'Armand.' She said it lightly, but she was aware of a growing sense of intimacy in their conversation which she wasn't sure she was ready to handle.

He shook his head. 'No, I will not be going.' He offered no further explanation, and to Gaby's irritation she realised that she was disappointed, that she had been hoping he was going to say he would be there. She was about to ask him if he knew Charles and Lisa Rayner, the couple who were holding the barbecue, but he spoke again before she had the chance.

'As you were not at the party last night, and the whole point of the party was for us to get to know you, maybe you could tell me something about yourself now.' Leaning back in his chair, he folded his arms and, crossing his ankles, rested his feet on a low stone wall that ran round the perimeter of the yard.

'I'm not sure there is a lot more to tell.' Gaby threw him a quick glance. 'You know I'm a widow, that I have a son. You know I work for OBEX, that I'm a nurse, but that I am now employed as a counsellor. . .even if that is something you are not in favour of—'

'I also know you have red hair,' he interrupted softly, 'and very white skin that burns in the sun. . .'

'So what else. . .?' She was laughing now at the gleam of amusement in his eyes.

'I want to know about you.' He half closed his eyes against the sunlight filtering through the silvery eucalyptus leaves. 'The person inside, what makes you the way you are.'

Embarrassed again, Gaby gave a little dismissive gesture with her hands.

But Armand was not to be dissuaded. 'What things do you like?' he persisted. 'What do you dislike? What are your hopes, your dreams?' He leaned forward. 'What are your fears?'

She knew he was watching her closely, so must have seen her look of surprise. Then he smiled and said, 'Ah, you wonder what right I have to want to know such things. Maybe you want to tell me to mind my own business. . .?'

She raised one eyebrow but he carried on regardless. 'We are to work together, Gabrielle.' He said it in a resigned sort of way, as if he had come to terms with her appointment at OBEX. 'We are to work closely with people who have problems—personal problems, many difficulties. . . So first, I think we need to know each other. . .do you not agree?'

'Yes,' Gaby replied slowly, 'if you put it like that, then I suppose we do. So, where shall I start?' She paused for a moment, reflecting, and from the coppice beyond the poppies they both heard the sound of the cuckoo. Armand remained silent, giving her time, and Gaby took a deep breath. 'I'm nearly thirty,' she said. 'I was born in a village just outside Branchester. I'm an only child. My father was a musician, my mother a teacher.'

'Musician?' His interest was further aroused.

Gaby nodded. 'Yes, he was a cellist.'

'Do you inherit his talent?'

'Not exactly, although I do play the piano and I adore music.' She paused reflectively. 'When my father was alive,' she continued after a moment, 'we went to every concert he took part in. After he died, my mother discouraged me from taking up music as a career. I suppose she'd had too many years of worrying about finance to see me take the same road.'

She fell silent again, then after a moment added, 'She's remarrying soon.' She said it almost as an afterthought, then found herself glancing quickly at Armand to see his reaction. When he raised his eyebrows in apparent interest, she said, 'To an old friend of my father's, actually. . .' She nodded. 'I'm pleased for her,' she said, after another brief silence, 'my father's been dead for eight years.'

'I would imagine you and your mother have been a comfort to each other, especially since your own husband died,' Armand said quietly.

'Yes.' Gaby nodded again. 'Yes, we have,' she admitted. 'In fact we've shared the same house. . . Now I'm not quite sure what will happen. . .' She trailed off, and to her horror felt sudden tears prick the back of her eyes.

'You mean you have no home?' She was aware of the surprised concern in his voice.

'Oh, no,' she said quickly. 'It isn't like that. My mother and Henry—he's the man she's going to marry—have made it quite plain that there is always a home with them for Oliver and myself. . .but. . .'

'You perhaps think otherwise?' he said softly.

'I think it will be better for them to be on their own,' replied Gaby. She paused, then, when Armand made no further comment, she went on, 'When this opportunity came up to work at the Toulouse factory I thought it could be the chance of a new life for Oliver and me.' She deliberately allowed a positive note to enter her voice.

'And Monsieur Jackson?' The question, coming after a brief but poignant silence, was casual, but Armand's tone somehow reflected a growing tension between them. 'Does he figure in this new life?'

While Gaby was searching to find the right words to answer his question Adèle appeared with coffee for them both.

'Thank you, Adèle.' Grateful for the interruption, Gaby took her cup and saucer and set it down on the stone wall beside her.

'I give Oliver his orange juice.' Adèle turned and went back into the house.

In the moments that followed Gaby hoped that Armand might have become sidetracked by the arrival of the coffee, because for some reason that she couldn't fully explain she found that she really didn't want to discuss her relationship with Martin.

'You were about to tell me where Monsieur Jackson figures in your plans for the future.' Armand spoke suddenly, setting his own cup down beside hers on the wall and at the same time dashing any hopes she might have had that he had lost the thread of their conversation.

'I think,' she replied, saying the first thing that came into her head, 'that at this moment I'm not absolutely sure.'

'And yet when I asked yesterday,' he replied softly, 'you confirmed the fact that he is your boyfriend.'

'Yes, yes, I did,' Gaby agreed. 'Although,' she added after a moment, 'if I remember rightly, that was your wording and not mine. I believe I referred to Martin as a friend—a good friend.'

He didn't respond immediately, instead picking up his cup and sipping his coffee, then carefully replacing the cup in the saucer. Gaby, watching him, was struck by the casual elegance of his clothes, by the expensive leather shoes and the gold-rimmed sunglasses protruding from the top pocket of his cream shirt.

At last he spoke. 'Was it his idea that you should join him in Toulouse?' he said.

Gaby hesitated, only too aware that she didn't want this man to gain the wrong impression. 'In a way,' she said at last, then, when Armand's expression remained inscrutable, she went on, 'At least, when the job came up Martin encouraged me to apply for it. He has been lodging in St Michel for about six months now. He likes it so much that he wants to buy a property and settle here.'

'And you?' He was watching her closely again. 'Do you like it so much that you want to settle here?'

'It is far too soon for me to say,' she protested, shifting restlessly on her chair. 'I haven't even started my job yet, and Oliver has to start school. . .'

'You are able to stay here?' He glanced round as he spoke, at the yard dappled with morning sunlight, then at the house.

Gaby nodded. 'Yes, we've been incredibly lucky. Penny and Tom have agreed that we can stay here for. . .' She paused. 'For as long as it takes to sort ourselves out,' she concluded. She didn't want to tell him that Martin wanted her to stay there only until he had bought his property, and that then the idea was that she and Oliver should move in with him. Instead, in a determined attempt to change the subject, she said, 'But that's quite enough about me—what about you?'

'Me?' He looked so surprised that she wondered if she'd overstepped the mark. He was, after all, in effect going to be her senior colleague. But by this time Gaby was almost past caring.

'That party had two functions you know,' she went on quickly. 'It wasn't just for everyone to get to know me. It was for me to get to know the people I shall be working with. I've told you about myself, now it's your turn. Have you always lived in Toulouse?' she asked boldly, before she had a chance to chicken out.

He glanced up sharply, as if he was surprised—either that she had asked or that she should want to know. Gaby wasn't sure which. Then he shrugged. 'More or less,' he said, then he added, 'At least, since I have been in practice. It is. . .how you say?. . .convenient?'

Gaby nodded, and as a mental picture came into her mind of that quiet courtyard and the elegant town house he continued. 'My family home is near Cordes, in the Gaillac region. My mother and my brother run the family business there.'

'Which is?' Gaby raised her eyebrows, her interest aroused.

'A vineyard,' he explained. 'It has been in my family for many generations.'

'And yet you are a doctor?' She was curious now.

He laughed, revealing very white teeth. 'Yes, yes,' he agreed, 'I am a doctor. . .much to the disapproval of my family. Being the eldest son, it was assumed I would take over the business. . . Instead, it is my brother Gérard and his wife Monique who help my mother.'

'While you are a doctor. . .' Gaby murmured, now even more intrigued by the situation.

'I knew when I was in my teens that the vineyard

wouldn't be enough for me,' he said after a moment. 'I had become bored with the whole business of the production of wine. . . Not that I don't enjoy wine,' he added quickly with a laugh, catching sight of Gaby's expression, 'quite the reverse—I greatly appreciate fine wines. But. . .' He shrugged in the nonchalant way she had come to associate with him in the brief time she had known him. 'I needed more. . .I like people, I care about people—they fascinate me.'

'Me too.' Gaby nodded. 'Especially the way people behave, and why they do so. There is always a reason for people's reactions to events in their lives and it is those reasons that intrigue me—I suppose that's why I enjoy my counselling work so much.'

'Ah, your work,' he said thoughtfully. 'In spite of my reservations about what you do, I have to admit I am sure you will find yourself in great demand at the factory.'

'Are you saying there is a lot of stress amongst the employees?'

He spread his hands, the gesture implying that he thought so but that she would have to draw her own conclusions.

They were silent for a moment as they finished their coffee, then, half teasingly, Gaby heard herself say, 'So what other likes do you have besides fine wines?'

He smiled—a lazy smile, almost intimate—and Gaby wished she hadn't asked.

'I too like music,' he said after a moment. 'And cars. Oh, and war games, I have to confess. I like war games.'

'War games?' She stared at him in amazement, wondering what he meant.

He nodded. 'I have an interest in battles and military strategy,' he said, appearing for a moment to be lost in thought, then abruptly he drained his cup and stood up. 'I have to go,' he said, and Gaby thought she detected a note of reluctance in his voice. 'I have calls to make,' he added by way of explanation.

Just for a moment she had forgotten that he was a doctor, presumably with house calls to make just like any other doctor. But maybe that was why she had forgotton, because that was where the similarity ended. For Armand Laurent, with his family background and his expensive tastes, wasn't like most of the GPs with whom Gaby came into contact.

She too stood up, then walked with him to the front of the house. In the forecourt an Italian sports car was parked, its black bodywork shining in the sun. Armand smiled when he saw Gaby's expression.

'I told you,' he said with a helpless shrug, 'cars are my weakness. . .or, at least, one of my weaknesses.'

'There are others?' She deliberately kept her tone light.

'One other,' he said softly.

'Which is?' she murmured, at the same time wondering how she had the nerve to ask, given the expression that had come into his eyes as he looked down at her.

'Pre-Raphaelite-type women with Titian hair.'

She felt the colour flood her cheeks, then with a wave of his hand he got into the car, shut the door and was gone—out of the gates and down the track to the road—while she stood watching him.

CHAPTER FOUR

'THIS will be your consulting room—I hope you like it.' Julie Roberts, the nursing Sister at the OBEX occupational medical centre, opened a door and stood back for Gaby to precede her into a light, airy room on the third floor.

'It's lovely.' Gaby looked round. The walls and carpet were plain but pleasing to the eye, in varying shades of apricot. A pine desk, complete with computer, together with a black leather chair were situated in front of the large picture window. Two comfortable armchairs covered in a rich cinnamon-coloured material faced the desk, while the walls were lined with filing cabinets, bookshelves and other essential office equipment. Someone had placed a couple of pot plants on one of the shelves beside a welcome-looking coffee-machine, and on the walls were a couple of good prints by Toulouse Lautrec.

Gaby strolled to the window and gazed out. Immediately below were the factory grounds and a new office block that was under construction, while beyond it seemed that the whole of Toulouse lay before her.

'What a view!' she said after a moment, turning to Julie.

'Yes, it is rather impressive, isn't it?' Julie smiled. 'But—like anything else—one gets used to it after a while.'

'Yes, I suppose so.' Gaby, who had turned back to the window, reluctantly tore her gaze away and looked at Julie again. 'How long have you been here?' she asked curiously.

'Nearly two years.'

'You quite obviously like it, if you've been here that long.'

Julie laughed and looped her straight blonde hair back behind one ear. 'The fact that I'm going to marry a Frenchman just might have something to do with that—but, yes, I do like it here. In fact, I love it.'

'You're getting married?' Gaby's eyes widened with interest.

'Yes.' Julie nodded. 'Jean Paul is a test pilot for OBEX. We met the day I arrived here.'

'How romantic!' Gaby smiled at Julie's obvious excitement.

'Your situation sounds pretty romantic as well,' said Julie, eyeing her speculatively.

'My situation?' Gaby had turned to the desk to inspect the computer, but she paused and looked sharply at Julie.

'Yes.' Julie appeared to hesitate for a moment, almost as if she was wondering if she'd said the right thing, then, when Gaby remained silent, waiting for her to continue, she hurriedly explained, 'I was talking to Martin Jackson last week at Mélisande's party, and he told me that he was looking for a property so that the two of you can be together.'

Gaby felt herself stiffen involuntarily. Was that what Martin had told everyone? That they were about to live together?

'Is there something wrong?' Julie was frowning. 'Have I said the wrong thing?'

'No, no—not really,' Gaby said quickly, not wanting to discuss Martin or their relationship with this girl, who, after all, was a stranger—nice as she might appear. And besides, had she not led Martin to believe that that was what would eventually happen? Wasn't that what she wanted?

'I think this counselling business is a brilliant idea.'

Julie was talking again, and Gaby forced herself to forget Martin and concentrate on what she was saying.

'I'm sure it will ease our workload on the medical unit. So many people we see are under such a lot of pressure, either from their work or from some domestic or personal problem, and we just don't have the time to listen to them.'

'That's what I'm here for,' said Gaby lightly, relieved that the subject had changed again.

'I understand you were involved in the same scheme at the Branchester factory?' asked Julie.

Gaby nodded. 'Yes, I worked with Dr David Markham and his wife Rachel, who pioneered the scheme. It was such a success it was decided to repeat it here.'

'Well, like I say—there'll be plenty for you to do,' said Julie. 'People are away from family and friends, strain is put on relationships, work performance suffers—oh, it all happens here, believe me!'

'Sounds like I'm going to have my work cut out—' Gaby broke off and looked up quickly as she realised that someone was standing in the open doorway. A slim, attractive, dark-haired woman, with large expressive eyes, stood there watching them.

Julie, sensing another person's presence, also turned to the door. 'Mélisande!' She turned to Gaby. 'You two haven't met yet, have you?'

Gaby shook her head. 'No,' she said, then she smiled. 'And I have an apology to make for not attending your party.'

'Ah, Madame Dexter—at last!' The finely sculptured, classically French face relaxed into a smile. 'I understand; your little boy—he ill. He is better now?'

'Yes, yes, thank you.' Gaby felt a stab of relief. For some reason, which she was at a loss to explain, she realised that she had been dreading meeting this Frenchwoman. But it seemed that her fears had been entirely unfounded, because on first acquaintance she seemed both friendly and utterly charming.

'I was hoping I would meet you at the barbecue the following night,' Gaby went on, 'but Lisa said you weren't able to go.'

'A previous engagement,' murmured Mélisande.

'It's impossible to attend everything,' said Julie. 'The social life is non-stop. . . Speaking of which—' she stared at Gaby '—was Martin all right after the barbecue? He rather overdid the red wine, I thought.'

Gaby pulled a face. 'Yes, he did rather,' she admitted. 'But he was OK.' She passed it off lightly, but at the same time she was only too aware that Martin had made something of a fool of himself at Charles and Lisa's barbecue, and she cringed with embarrassment at the memory.

'Well, this won't do.' Julie sighed. 'I must go and do some work. We'll leave you to settle in, Gaby. Give us a buzz on here—' she touched an intercom button beside the telephone '—if there's anything you need.' She and Mélisande turned to go. 'Oh. . .' She paused. 'One other thing—if you'd like to come down in about—' she glanced at her watch '—an hour or so, I'll introduce you to Dr Laurent. He should be here by then.' She turned again to follow Mélisande out of the door.

'I've already met Dr Laurent,' said Gaby.

Julie turned in surprise, and Mélisande, who had opened the door, stopped, one hand on the door-handle.

'Have you?' said Julie, then as Gaby nodded she added, 'As you weren't at Mélisande's party I assumed. . .' She trailed off, frowning.

'We met at his house—or rather his surgery,' explained Gaby. 'My son, Oliver, had his asthma attack while we were in town, and Martin took us to Dr Laurent's. And then the next day Dr Laurent came to Penny Shackleton's—where we are staying—to visit Oliver.'

'Oh. . .' Julie sounded deflated, as if she had been hoping to be the one to effect the introductions. 'Oh, well, never mind. Maybe you'd better come down anyway—just for a chat. I understand you won't be seeing any patients today.'

'I thought I would spend today familiarising myself with the place, then I shall be available tomorrow to anyone who wants to talk.' Gaby kept her tone lighthearted, and, although Julie smiled in response, Mélisande, who had kept very still for the last minute or so, left the room without looking back.

As the door closed behind them Gaby turned to her desk, and with a sigh began unpacking her books and folders.

She worked steadily for the next half-hour, arranging

the office to suit herself. At the very bottom of her briefcase was a photograph in a silver frame. Gaby drew it out and stood looking at it for a long moment, then carefully she positioned it on her desk so that both Oliver and Terry would be right there with her as she worked.

For the hundredth time that morning she wondered how Oliver was getting on at school. He had been looking forward to going with Harry, Sam and Charlotte to the convent school just outside St Michel, but that morning he had been apprehensive, and Gaby had feared that the tension might bring on another asthma attack.

'He'll be all right.' Penny had tried to reassure her. 'I think it best if I take him. You've already explained to the Mother Superior about his medication, haven't you?'

She hadn't given Gaby time to protest, whisking Oliver away in her car along with her own children, leaving Gaby to go into Toulouse with Martin.

'I shall have to get transport of my own,' she'd said as she'd sat beside Martin in his car.

'There's no hurry.' He shrugged. 'After all, I do go to the factory every day.'

'We won't always be working the same hours,' Gaby reasoned quietly, 'and besides, my own car would be useful.'

He didn't reply, appearing to concentrate on the traffic as he joined the autoroute into Toulouse. Gaby had already thought that he seemed quiet, moody, even, that morning, and had decided it best to let him come round in his own time. He didn't speak again until he'd parked the car in the factory car park, then, as she got out and closed her door, he looked at her across the roof of the car.

'I'll ring the agent today about viewing that property,' he said. 'It sounds as if it could be just the sort of thing I'm looking for.' They began to cross the car park, waiting for two lorries delivering materials to the building site to pass. 'I'll try and arrange a time we can both go to see it,' he added.

They climbed the short flight of steps in front of the main entrance, then Martin stopped before the double glass doors and looked at Gaby. 'Do you know where you have to go?' he asked.

She nodded and pointed to a noticeboard where a red arrow pointed in the direction of the medical unit.

'Well, in that case. . .' Martin gave a vague nod. 'I'll leave you to it—see you later.' He turned to go, then, as an obvious afterthought, looked over his shoulder and said, 'Hope you get on OK.'

'Thanks, Martin.'

As she'd watched him stride off down the corridor to the design offices she'd found herself thinking once more how like Terry he was.

And now, as she gazed down at Terry's photograph, she thought it again—so like Terry and yet. . . It was strange, uncanny at times. . . She found herself expecting him to behave in a certain way, or to react to a situation in the way she knew Terry would have done, and then having to remind herself, when Martin's responses were quite the opposite, that he was not Terry.

The likeness to her late husband had been what had attracted her to Martin Jackson in the first place— Gaby was well aware of that. The blue eyes, fresh complexion, the wheat-coloured hair and the well-built physique had all jolted her into awareness when he had burst into the medical unit at Branchester late one afternoon.

Gaby, who had just been coming out of her consulting room had stopped in shock when she'd caught sight of him.

'Hi!' he said. 'Haven't seen you before. Are you one of the nurses?'

Numbly Gaby shook her head, then, recovering from the initial shock of his likeness to Terry, she said, 'Did you want to see a nurse?'

'Good God, no.' He looked horrified. 'Do I look ill?'

'No,' she admitted. 'But then not everyone does. . .'

'I've come to see Greg Bradshaw—the paramedic—

to arrange a game of squash. Nothing more sinister than that.'

'Oh, I see.' She smiled. 'He isn't here at the moment, I'm afraid.'

'Never mind.' He grinned. 'I'll talk to you instead.'

'I was just thinking of going to the canteen for a cup of tea,' she protested mildly.

'In that case, mind if I join you?'

'No, of course not.' And she meant it. Her heart was still thumping from the shock of his resemblance to Terry, and she was suddenly eager to find out more about him. Her reaction took her by surprise, because she had allowed no one else into her life since losing Terry, had not wanted anyone else. Now, here was this slightly brash, forthright man, who, if the look in his eyes was anything to go by, quite obviously found her attractive and wanted to get to know her better.

And over the next few weeks that was what had happened. They'd gone out together—to pubs, to clubs, for walks in the country with Oliver and her mother's golden retriever, Chamois, to football matches and to the swimming baths—and at first Gaby had found herself living on some sort of high as she'd tried to come to terms with the unbelievable fact that she'd found someone like Terry.

After Martin's transfer, albeit at his suggestion, she had even found herself applying for the post in Toulouse, then, much to her surprise, being offered the job and agreeing to move to France to see how things would work out.

And here she was. She looked round at her new consulting room again, this time with a steadily growing sense of satisfaction. She was making new friends, and Oliver seemed happy.

It was a start. If she was honest, she wasn't yet completely sure where her relationship with Martin was leading—but surely, she thought, as she turned and looked out over the pink-bricked city again, time would be the judge of that.

For the moment she needed to concentrate on the present, which meant her new job and the people she would be working with. Maybe, she mused, she should go down to the medical unit, familiarise herself with the surroundings and get to know the staff.

The staff.

That meant the unit nurses, the paramedics and. . .and the doctor.

Julie had said that Dr Laurent would be there. Gaby felt her heart miss a beat as she recalled the look in his eyes when he had told her he would call her Gabrielle instead of Gaby, and then again, later, when he had likened her to a Pre-Raphaelite woman.

He was charming, there was no doubt about that, and she was unfamiliar with that type of charm.

'Smooth', Martin had called him, lumping him together with all Frenchmen.

Well, maybe he was.

But it was nice. Gaby smiled with pleasure at the memories, and was still smiling as someone tapped on her door and pushed it open.

And suddenly, as if simply thinking of him had conjured him up, there he was before her—and she was still smiling.

A quizzical look came into his dark eyes. 'Am I interrupting?' he said softly.

'No.' Gaby shook her head. 'No, of course not. Please, come in.'

'But you were laughing.'

'I was smiling,' she replied. 'It is a different thing altogether.'

'The memory of something amused you?'

'Pleased, more than amused,' she admitted.

They stared at each other for a long moment, and Gaby had the distinct impression that Armand knew exactly what she had been smiling about.

In the end she was forced to lower her gaze. 'I was about to come and find you,' she said lightly.

'Really?' He sounded both pleased and intrigued by the prospect.

'I thought it was high time I found out about my colleagues and my work.'

'Ah, work.' He paused. 'And there was I thinking it was me you wanted to see.'

She didn't reply—couldn't reply. Instead she found herself taking a mental note of his beautifully cut eau-de-Nil linen jacket, with its hand-stitched finish, and the matching chinos in a slightly darker tone. The overall effect was understated, elegant, but at the same time intensely masculine.

'How is Oliver?' he asked, when it became apparent that she wasn't going to compromise herself further.

'He is well, thank you.' She inclined her head, suddenly overwhelmingly pleased that she had chosen to wear the cream cotton skirt and lacy top that she knew accentuated her colouring so well. 'He's started school today,' she added. 'I hope he's coping. . .'

'I am sure he is.' Armand inclined his head slightly. 'I rather feel he has the same courage as his mother.'

'Courage?' Her head jerked up quickly, in surprise. 'I wouldn't say I was particularly courageous.'

'No?' He raised his eyebrows, and the silence in the room suddenly seemed heightened while the sounds beyond the plate glass window—of workmen, of river boats and of aircraft leaving or taking off from Toulouse Airport—seemed very, very far away, almost to belong to another world. 'It takes courage to bring yourself and your child to a strange country on your own,' he said at last.

Gaby gave a light shrug. 'Well, I wasn't exactly alone. . .' she murmured.

'Ah,' Armand said softly, 'I was forgetting—Monsieur Jackson?'

'Yes.' She nodded, wishing that he hadn't mentioned Martin, then immediately hating herself for it. After all, if it hadn't been for Martin it was highly unlikely that she would be in France at all. 'Yes, it's all down to Martin really,' she said weakly.

'Surely not entirely.' Armand was frowning now, his gaze sweeping the room. 'I would think your own expertise came into it somewhere. Monsieur Jackson can hardly be responsible for your psychology and counselling experience.'

'Maybe not,' Gaby agreed. 'But he organised our accommodation with Penny and Tom, helped us with the move—and I mustn't lose sight of the fact that it was his idea in the first place that I should apply for the post.'

'Really?' Armand's reply, though polite, appeared uninterested, as if Martin's part in events was of little consequence to him. He stopped his perusal of the room and Gaby realised that his gaze had come to rest on the photograph on her desk. Leaning forward, he picked it up, and as he studied it Gaby watched his face. His expression remained inscrutable, and after a moment, without a word, he replaced the picture.

Gaby found herself fighting a feeling of disappointment. She realised that she had wanted him to comment on Terry—to say something, anything, even if it was only something on the lines of Oliver's resemblance to his father.

Instead, he said, 'So you were coming to find me to talk about work?'

She nodded, relieved now that the conversation was switching away from personal matters. 'Yes, I thought we should discuss the types of cases you will be referring to me for counselling.'

He was staring at her again, and she felt a sudden wave of panic.

'That's assuming, of course, that you actually intend referring anyone?' She tried to keep the question light, casual, but there was underlying anxiety in her tone and she knew from his expression that he had detected it.

'You think I may not?' he murmured softly, his eyes not leaving her face.

Quite suddenly Gaby realised that her knees had grown weak and were threatening to give way. She sat down heavily in the leather chair behind her desk, desperately trying to concentrate on their conversation and to ignore the look in his eyes.

'You have already made it plain you are not in favour of counselling,' she said stiffly, then, regaining her confidence, went on, 'Not that you're by any means the first doctor of my experience to be oblivious to its advantages—'

To her dismay Armand laughed. 'So what happened to them, these other sceptics?' he asked. 'Did you win them over in the end?'

'It was more a case of them being grateful for the easing of their workloads,' she retorted, feeling her colour rising.

'I am all in favour of anything that will ease my workload—and as to the advantages of counselling—' he shrugged '—maybe we should simply let time be the judge of that.'

'So can I expect referrals?'

'Of course,' he said, sitting on the edge of her desk. 'If the facility is there I would be a fool not to make use of you.'

Gaby looked up swiftly, her eyes meeting his. She was not sure she wanted to be likened to a facility, or to be made use of, yet on the other hand she knew that she could be in trouble if he refused to acknowledge the service she was offering. Calmly she managed to hold his gaze, but her pulse began racing as she considered the full implications in what he had just said. Maybe his choice of words was ambiguous, or perhaps some meaning was changed in the translation, but, whatever it was, it stirred all manner of emotions deep inside her.

She swallowed, then made a show of standing up and putting some papers away in the desk drawer in an attempt to hide these disconcerting feelings.

He too stood up then, and, as if he was fully aware of her discomfort, said, 'Why don't you come down with me now to the medical unit, and meet the rest of the staff?'

She nodded, not trusting her voice, while Armand moved to the door and opened it, standing aside so that she could precede him into the corridor. The space was confined, and as she passed him her shoulder brushed lightly against his chest. In the same instant he lowered his head, and she caught the scent of some expensive cologne as, for the most fleeting of moments, his face touched the soft cloud of her hair.

Then the moment was gone. Armand closed the door behind him, and as they began walking down the corridor towards the distant but unmistakable sounds of the factory Gaby wondered if she had imagined it.

Moments later they descended the stairs and entered the factory, and if Gaby hadn't known otherwise she could easily have believed she was back in Branchester. The noise level was certainly the same—almost deafening with the sounds of hammering, of drilling, of the shouts of the men, of whistling, of laughter. It looked the same too, with the overhead jigs on differing floor levels linked by metal stairways, the hydraulic lifts, the massive cranes and the half-assembled sections of aircraft like the skeletons of prehistoric monsters.

Taking up one entire wall were the design shops and administration offices overlooking the shop floor, fronted by acres of glass. And there was the workforce itself—the men on the shop floor in their familiar royal blue overalls with the word 'OBEX' on the breast pocket, and the design staff and management in white shirts and grey suits.

The only difference from Branchester, as far as Gaby could make out, was that some of the employees were French, some German and some Italian, and as she and Armand walked through the factory snatches of the different languages reached her ears.

Armand led the way to the medical unit which, thankfully, was soundproofed, and as he shut the door behind them he pulled a rueful face and said, 'Perhaps now we can hear ourselves see.'

Gaby smiled. 'Don't you mean think?' she said.

'I am sorry?' For a moment Armand looked bewildered. It was the first time Gaby had seen him anything less than in total control, and she found the situation oddly comforting.

'You said, "Perhaps now we can hear ourselves see",' she explained patiently, watching his face as she spoke. 'The expression you wanted was, hear ourselves *think*.'

'Ah!' His face cleared. 'I am sorry. It is my English. It is not always good.'

'You speak excellent English,' she replied quickly. 'I only wish my French was as good.'

'You speak my language?' His voice softened and his eyes met hers.

'Yes,' Gaby admitted, 'but badly. Only schoolgirl stuff, really. I need some lessons.'

'Hélène would teach you,' he said quickly.

'Hélène?' She frowned; she couldn't remember meeting anyone of that name, yet Armand had spoken as if she should know.

'You met her,' he said. 'At my house in town.'

Gaby had a mental picture of the tall, rather gaunt woman who had opened the door of the house in the courtyard. 'She teaches French?' she asked.

Armand nodded, then looked up as Julie Roberts came out of a room at the far end of the unit. 'Yes,' he murmured, 'she used to be a teacher, now she is. . .my. . .' He searched for a word.

'Secretary?' asked Gaby, and when he still looked hesitant she went on, 'Receptionist? Housekeeper?'

Armand laughed. 'A bit of all three, perhaps. She looks after me—tells me where I should be.' He turned to Julie then, and Gaby found herself wondering about the other woman who had been in Armand's house, the woman whose laughter she had heard, whose perfume had lingered in the air. At the time she had wondered if it had been his wife, but if that was the case, and he *was* married, would he need the rather formidable Hélène to look after him?

She had no time to speculate further, because Julie, looking almost accusingly at Armand, said, 'I wondered where you were.' At the same time she shot Gaby a curious glance, implying that it was her fault that the doctor had gone missing. 'It's almost time for surgery,' she went on, defending her attitude.

Armand shrugged, apparently unperturbed. 'I bring Gabrielle here. I think she should see the unit and meet the others.'

'Well, yes, of course.' Julie looked a bit flustered. 'I was intending to do the same, but I thought she would like to settle into her room first.'

Gaby, feeling sorry for her, came to her rescue. 'Julie had already suggested I come down to the unit after I sorted my room out,' she said quickly, then added, 'Talking of my room—isn't it rather a long way from the unit?'

'That was deliberate,' explained Julie as she turned and led the way into the unit's reception area. 'We thought it might be better for your patients if they could come and talk to you in complete privacy, well away from the factory and the treatment rooms. We thought it might encourage them to talk about their problems, didn't we, Armand?' She turned anxiously to the doctor.

He nodded. 'We did,' he replied. 'But if you are unhappy with the arrangement, I am sure we can find somewhere else for you. . .'

'Oh, no.' Gaby hastened to reassure them. 'My room is fine. And I think your idea is excellent. From my experience I know only too well that privacy gains peoples' confidence.'

'I think Gabrielle was afraid we might forget her presence and not refer patients to her,' said Armand teasingly.

Julie rolled her eyes and glanced through a glass partition to the rapidly filling waiting room. 'There's no fear of that. We simply don't have the time to do more than offer hands-on treatment. There are so many times when we know that people simply want someone to talk to, to unload some of their stress, but we have to hurry them along. I shall certainly refer patients to you, Gaby—you need have no fears on that score.'

Armand smiled, but did not comment.

'In fact—' Julie lowered her voice so that only the three of them could hear '—I've already seen we have Lisa Rayner on the list. I think she might be one to benefit from talking to Gaby. What do you say, Armand?'

Armand shrugged. 'Yes,' he agreed at last—almost reluctantly, Gaby thought. 'I suppose she could.'

'Lisa Rayner?' said Gaby quickly. 'Do you mean Charles Rayner's wife?'

Julie nodded. 'Yes.' She paused. 'Have you met her, Gaby?'

'Yes, I was invited to a barbecue at their house the other night.' She glanced quickly from Julie to Armand, then back to Julie again. 'Does she work here?' she asked curiously.

'No.' Julie shook her head then added, 'But, as you know, we treat employees' families as well as the employees themselves—especially the British ones.'

'I see.' Gaby glanced at Armand. 'Well, I will be glad to talk to Lisa if you think I may be of help.'

'I will suggest it to her and see if she agrees.' He gave rather a curt little nod, and Gaby found herself thinking that she could be in for something of a battle with him over his attitude towards recommending patients for counselling.

Julie glanced at the fob watch pinned to the front of her dark blue uniform. 'We've got ten minutes,' she said. 'Come into the staff room and meet Suzanne—she's the other nurse on duty today—and Luc, who's our paramedic. And if we look sharp I would say there's time for a quick coffee before we start.'

Gaby and Armand followed Julie through the unit, past two large treatment rooms, the rest rooms, the stores, and finally into the staff room. A long, narrow room, it ran the length of the unit and overlooked the factory grounds and car parks.

Julie introduced Gaby to Suzanne, an Englishwoman like herself, who had settled in France, and to Luc, a young French paramedic, whose command of the English language put Gaby to shame and even further strengthened her resolve to do something about improving her French.

While Julie was pouring coffee from a filter machine into pottery mugs Armand took a telephone call that came through for him from the main switchboard. Suzanne and Luc finished their own coffee and then left the staff room to return to the treatment room.

Gaby, meanwhile, wandered to the window.

In the distance, beyond the factory grounds, she could see the runways of Toulouse Airport. The bright morning sunlight glinted on the metalwork of the aircraft awaiting take off and even as Gaby watched one of the planes moved away from the rest, taxied, gathered speed and finally took off into the blue.

Usually when she saw an aeroplane Gaby found herself wishing that she was aboard.

Did she wish that she was on that one? Did she wish that she was on her way back to England?

She turned at a slight sound behind her. Armand was still talking on the phone, but his gaze met hers and in that instant she knew without doubt that she was glad she wasn't on that aircraft, glad that she was here in Toulouse, about to make a fresh start in her life.

'We have an emergency coming up from the factory floor.' Armand appeared to drag his gaze away from Gaby to Julie.

'What is it?' asked Julie.

'A flash from welding has caught a man's eyes,' replied Armand briefly as he strode towards the door.

Julie, about to follow him, paused and looked at Gaby. 'Want to come?' she said.

'Yes, please.' Gaby set her mug down and hurried to join them. It would be interesting to see how they dealt with the emergency.

The man, an Englishman in his early thirties, was lying on a couch in one of the treatment rooms. He was in a great deal of pain and Julie had difficulty in persuading him even to allow Armand to examine his eyes. Eventually Armand was able to insert soothing drops, to help calm the intense inflammation from the flash.

'What happens now, Doc?' the man gasped as the drops gradually began to take effect. 'Will my sight be OK?'

'I want you to see an eye specialist,' Armand replied. 'Sister Roberts will arrange for you to be taken to the hospital.'

While Julie went away to make the necessary

arrangements Armand made another attempt at an examination. After a moment he turned, as if looking for something. Gaby, who was watching, leaned forward. 'Can I help?' she said quietly.

Armand didn't reply immediately, instead continuing to peer into the man's eyes. When at last he did straighten up he turned, but without looking at Gaby, and said, 'I hardly think this is a case for counselling. What this man needs is specialised medical treatment.'

Gaby flinched, and in that instant she knew that in spite of his earlier assurance that he *would* use the service she would provide, and refer patients to her, she really did have a long way to go to prove the merits of her job to this man. That it was going to be a challenge she had little doubt. . .but Gaby had always been one to rise to a challenge. And this situation, she resolved silently as the ambulance arrived to take the injured man to the hospital, was quite definitely not going to be an exception.

CHAPTER FIVE

BY THE end of her first week at the factory Gaby was beginning to feel as if she'd lived in France all her life. She settled quickly into a routine, and what started as a slight trickle of patients quickly became a steady flow as the nurses on the unit discovered the benefits of her experience and began to refer patients suffering from stress-related conditions. Armand was slower to respond, but Gaby was prepared for that and knew she would have to work just that bit harder where he was concerned.

One of those to talk to her, at Julie Roberts' suggestion, was Lisa Rayner. She came to see Gaby one afternoon at the end of that week, following an appointment with Armand. She was a pretty, dark-haired girl, with very blue eyes and a naturally high colour, but as she entered her consulting room Gaby could not help but notice how drawn and tired she looked.

'Hello, Lisa.' Gaby stood up and welcomed her, indicated for her to take a seat, then poured coffee for them both.

Lisa seemed nervous and ill at ease, and Gaby knew from experience that because they had already met in a social capacity it could prove difficult to win her confidence. She had also learnt during a preliminary discussion with Armand that Lisa was taking prescribed anti-depressants.

'I didn't know you did this sort of thing.' Lisa perched on the very edge of one of the armchairs, her gaze darting round Gaby's room.

'What sort of thing?' Gaby smiled as she turned from the coffee-machine and handed Lisa her coffee.

'This. . .sorting out peoples' problems. . .' Lisa's hand shook slightly and the cup rattled in the saucer.

'Well, I wouldn't say I actually sort out peoples'

problems.' Gaby set her own cup and saucer down on the desk. 'Only people themselves can do that,' she added. Moving round behind the desk again, she sat down, then, leaning forward and putting her elbows on the desk, she rested her chin on her hands and said, 'But I'm a good listener.'

'I see.' Lisa put her cup and saucer down too. 'When you first arrived I thought you were a nurse.'

'Actually, I am a nurse.'

'Are you?' Lisa looked up quickly, then she frowned. 'So why are you doing this?'

'I've been a counsellor for several years now,' replied Gaby. 'It's something that is becoming increasingly recognised by the medical profession—either as an alternative, or as therapy to work in conjunction with medication.'

'I'm on medication.' Lisa's voice shook slightly. 'I've been depressed,' she added.

'Do you know why?' asked Gaby gently.

'Not really.' Lisa shrugged. 'Everyone tells me I've got nothing to be depressed about. I've got a husband who loves me, a lovely home and a good job—I've been told on more than one occasion that I should pull myself together and count my blessings.'

Gaby pulled a face. 'Wonderful advice if you can do it. But let's face it—if you could, you wouldn't have gone to a doctor in the first place, or be sitting here now talking to me.'

'Exactly,' Lisa replied wryly.

'Tell me a bit about yourself,' said Gaby after a moment, taking her elbows from the desk and leaning back in her chair.

'What do you want to know?'

'Everything you can think of.' Gaby nodded encouragingly, then, when she saw Lisa's confused expression, she said, 'I only know that you are married to Charles and that you have that lovely home I visited the other day. Tell me, for example, how old you are, where you were born, how long you've been in France.'

Lisa, still frowning, took a sip of her coffee. 'Well,' she began hesitantly, 'I'm twenty-eight. I was born in

Leeds and I've been in France for two years.'

'How long have you and Charles been married?'

'Just over three years.'

'You said you have a good job? Who do you work for?'

'I'm self-employed.'

'Really?' Gaby was surprised. For some reason she had imagined Lisa to be in an administrative post. 'What do you do?'

'I make jewellery,' Lisa replied, and there was no disguising the note of pride that crept into her voice. 'I work from home,' she added.

'How exciting.' Gaby stared at her. 'Is that one of your pieces?' Leaning forward, she pointed to a silver pendant set with tiny turquoise beads that Lisa was wearing on a thin strip of leather round her neck.

'Yes.' Lisa nodded.

'It's beautiful,' said Gaby. 'I've been admiring it ever since you came into the room. Where do you sell your work?'

'In a craft shop near the cathedral.'

'I must go and have a look—I should like to see more,' said Gaby.

Lisa looked pleased and sat further back in her chair.

'Why do you come here to see a doctor?' asked Gaby after a moment.

'Charles suggested I came here to see Dr Laurent,' Lisa replied. 'He'd seen him himself on a couple of occasions and, well, it seemed the obvious thing to do. I think all the families of the OBEX employees do that,' she added as an afterthought.

Gaby nodded. 'So I understand, and I must admit it makes sense for all the members of one family to see the same doctor.' She paused, then very casually she said, 'No plans to increase the size of your family?'

Lisa shook her head. 'No,' she said quickly, then, correcting herself, went on, 'At least, not immediately... We do both want children,' she hastened to add, 'but not just yet... We think we need to get on our feet first and, well, Charles is working hard for promotion...'

'Yes, I understand.' Gaby nodded. 'So tell me a bit about this depression,' she went on after a moment.

Lisa's face took on the guarded expression that had been there before she had started talking about her work, and for some considerable time she remained silent. Then at last, slowly, she said, 'To tell you the truth, at first I didn't even know it was depression—I could hardly believe it when Dr Laurent prescribed anti-depressants for me.'

'Tell me about your symptoms,' said Gaby.

'They were strange, really. . .' Lisa paused, reflecting deeply.

'Can you remember how it started?'

'Not being able to sleep,' she replied hesitantly, then more positively she added, 'Yes, that was the first thing—not being able to sleep.'

'When you say not being able to sleep, do you mean you couldn't get off to sleep?' asked Gaby.

'Sometimes.' Lisa moved to the edge of her seat again and began twisting her wedding ring round and round. 'Then, at other times,' she went on, 'I would go off all right then wake up after only a couple of hours. I would start thinking. . .jumbled thoughts. . . all sorts of things. . .then I wouldn't be able to get back to sleep.' She paused, frowning. 'Sometimes I would sleep most of the night but wake very early—' She broke off and glanced at Gaby, then when Gaby remained silent she went on.

'The next thing was that I seemed to lose my appetite. . .and I started losing weight. At first I was pleased, because I had put on a few pounds since I'd got married, but then it reached the stage where none of my clothes seemed to fit. . . Then, to crown it all, I began to have panic attacks whenever I was away from the house for more than an hour or so. It got so bad that I dreaded going anywhere, and you know what it's like here. . .the social life. . .' She trailed off, then in sudden desperation she said, 'I didn't even want to take my jewellery into the shop in Toulouse—I was getting Charles to do it for me. . .'

Gaby got up, crossed the room and poured more

coffee for them both, then, when she'd returned to her seat, she said, 'When you wake in the night, Lisa, what do you think about?'

'I told you. . .it's all jumbled.'

'You can't remember anything specific?'

Lisa was silent for a moment, then she said, 'Dark thoughts. . .that's what they are. Black. Morbid things.' She shuddered. 'I can't talk about them.'

'OK,' said Gaby lightly, 'let's talk about Charles instead.'

'Charles. . .?' Lisa looked up quickly.

'Yes—where did you meet him?'

'When I was at art college he was at the university— we met in a local pub where all the students used to go.'

'Was this in Leeds?'

Lisa nodded.

Gaby remained silent, guessing that for the moment Lisa's thoughts were right back there in those early, carefree days. 'So is Charles a Leeds boy?' she asked after a moment.

'Oh, no,' Lisa said quickly. 'He came from down south—Surrey.'

'I see, so Charles had left home. What about you?'

'Me?' Lisa frowned.

'Yes.' Gaby nodded. 'Did you live in at art college?'

'No, there was no hall of residence. I lived at home until Charles and I married.'

'So has living here in France been the first time you've lived away from your family?'

'Except for the flat we lived in near Branchester when we were first married.'

'Did your family visit you very much at your flat?'

'Oh, yes, it wasn't too far away. . . My mother used to come over—she and I would go shopping together, have a bit of lunch. . .' She trailed off.

'Tell me about your family, Lisa.' Gaby sat back in her chair and crossed her legs.

Lisa shrugged. 'Not a lot to tell, really,' she said. 'I have one older brother, Craig—he's a computer programmer. My father has recently taken early retirement, he was a bank manager. . .'

'And your mother?'

'My mother?'

'Yes, what does she do?'

Lisa leaned forward in her chair, and Gaby noticed that her hands had curled into tight little fists.

'My mother is dead,' she said abruptly.

'Oh, I'm sorry,' said Gaby in surprise, then, when it seemed as if Lisa was not going to offer any further information, she said gently, 'When did she die, Lisa?'

'A year ago.' It came out as barely more than a whisper, and when Lisa raised her head, Gaby saw the gleam of tears in her eyes.

The silence in the room was broken only by the faint, distant sounds of the factory and the more immediate ticking of the clock on the wall facing the desk. Then, softly, and very gently, Gaby said, 'Tell me about your mother, Lisa.'

Later, when Lisa had gone after making another appointment for the following week, Gaby made her way down to the medical unit. She was feeling drained, as she usually did after an intensely emotional session with a patient.

'So how have you survived your first week?' Julie Roberts was in the treatment room and she looked up as Gaby appeared.

'Pretty well, I think.' Gaby eased herself up to sit on the side of an examination couch.

'It's always bewildering at first in any new job,' said Julie, 'let alone in a new country.'

'Yes.' Gaby nodded, absent-mindedly watching Julie as she packed instruments and dressings away.

'I've just been doing hearing tests,' Julie explained. 'The noise levels get so high that we constantly have to monitor peoples' hearing. Have you finished for today?' she added suddenly.

'I think so,' Gaby replied, then added, 'Unless Armand has anything for me.'

'Oh, talking of Armand—' Julie looked round quickly '—he was looking for you just now.'

'Was he?' Gaby was aware of a slight quickening of

her pulse. 'In that case he may well have a patient for me.'

Julie shut the door of the supplies cupboard. 'I dare say the problems you are dealing with are somewhat different from the ones you were used to in Branchester,' she said.

'Oh, I don't know,' Gaby replied. 'People are people, and, human nature being what it is, problems are much the same whether you are in an English country village or at the North Pole.'

'I hadn't thought of it like that,' said Julie slowly. 'But it seems to me the main problems here are caused by loneliness, differences in background and culture, and possibly the easy availability of alcohol.'

'All of which can lead to the kind of problems one encounters anywhere,' said Gaby.

'Yes, I suppose you're right,' Julie agreed, glancing up as the treatment room door suddenly opened. 'Oh, here's Armand now,' she said. 'I was just telling Gaby you were looking for her earlier,' she explained.

Gaby slid off the couch and Armand, who apparently hadn't immediately realised she was in the room, turned sharply to face her. 'Ah, here you are,' he said softly, and there was no disguising the sudden flare of pleasure in his eyes.

Gaby swallowed. 'You have a patient for me?' she said.

'No.' He shook his head. 'I would say you have coped with more than enough for your first week. I was wondering if you would like to come and see Hélène, to arrange some lessons?'

'Oh!' She stared stupidly at him. Go to his home? That beautiful courtyard? 'N-n-now?' she stammered, painfully aware that Julie was staring from one to the other of them with barely concealed curiosity.

'Yes.' He nodded, then paused. 'There is a problem?' he asked, raising his eyebrows.

'Not exactly. . .' She glanced at her watch.

'Oliver. . .?' he said quickly.

'No, Penny's picking him up from school. . .'

'Then. . .?'

'I have arranged to meet Martin at five o'clock.' Even to herself her voice sounded small, apologetic.

'We have plenty of time.' Armand made the decision for her. 'We go now,' he added, turning and opening the door for her. 'I get you back here for five.'

Hardly daring to look at Julie, she put her head down and hurried from the room.

The black Italian sports car was parked in the factory car park, and as Armand opened the door for her and Gaby slid into the passenger seat she had the distinct impression that she was being watched. Armand closed the door, and in the space of time it took for him to walk round to his own side of the car Gaby glanced up at the office windows that overlooked the car park. The blinds were down, protecting the rooms from the sun, but she still felt that eyes were watching.

Was it Martin, standing there in one of those offices watching them?

But what if he was? Gaby reasoned with herself. There was nothing wrong in what she was doing. Armand Laurent, although not exactly her boss, was her senior colleague, and what he was doing by arranging French lessons was helping to make life easier for her.

In spite of that, Gaby was distinctly relieved when Armand at last started the engine and they drew smartly away from the car park and away from the rows of blank office windows.

They took the main route, away from the industrial areas and the airport, following the curve of the river into the city. Armand drove fast, but his driving was skilful, full of confidence, his respect for the high-powered vehicle only too apparent.

The main routes were still busy, but Armand soon left those and entered the maze of back streets and alleys that surrounded the city centre. It was quieter here, for it was past midday and shutters had been fastened and shops closed as the sun beat relentlessly down and the heat bounced off the pavements.

More than once Gaby allowed herself a sideways glance at the man by her side. His face was set as he concentrated on the twists and turns of the narrow streets, and for the most part he remained silent. Once, she ventured to break the silence, asking if Hélène knew that she was coming.

Armand shook his head. 'No,' he said, then, apparently sensing her surprised reaction, added, 'But I have already asked her about lessons.'

'And what did she say?' asked Gaby curiously.

He gave a slight shrug. 'She is quite happy.'

Gaby bit her lip. She had the sudden, intuitive impression that the Frenchwoman had been anything but happy, but valued her job too much to say so. 'So why are we going to see her now?' she asked after a moment.

Armand answered, still keeping his eyes firmly on the road. 'To arrange a time convenient. . .' He hesitated. 'Convenient is the right word?' he asked, and when Gaby nodded he went on, 'Convenient to both of you.'

'I see.'

'I suggest at least twice a week,' Armand continued after a moment.

'It could be difficult,' murmured Gaby, trying desperately to ignore the stirring of excitement at the very thought of spending so much time at his lovely home.

'Difficult? Why difficult?' He threw her a sidelong glance then with a muttered exclamation slowed the car, swerving to avoid a black cat that streaked in front of them then bolted over the top of a high wall.

'Well, there's my job. . .' she began.

'You are not at the factory every hour of the day and night,' he replied smoothly.

'No,' she agreed. 'But when I am not at work, I like to spend my time with Oliver.'

'That is not a problem,' he said.

She threw him another glance and saw that he was smiling. 'It isn't. . .?' she said faintly, wondering how she could make him understand the importance of the time she spent with her son.

'No,' he said firmly. 'It is not a problem, because if necessary you will bring Oliver with you. He can stay with you during your lessons if he wishes, or he can spend the time with me.'

'With you?' Her eyes widened.

'Yes. Is that so improbable?'

'Well, no, I suppose not. . .it's just that. . .' She found herself floundering.

'I like children. . .and I particularly like Oliver,' he said. 'I do not have children of my own. I spend time with my brother's sons when I can, which is not as often as I would like.'

Once again Gaby found herself wondering if he was married, if that elusive woman who had been in his house on that first occasion had been his wife. Nothing had been said at the factory about his marital status, and Gaby had not quite been able to bring herself to ask anyone. Maybe there was a part of her that didn't want to know the answer. Maybe that was why she didn't just ask him now.

Which really was quite ridiculous, she thought as Armand slowed the car and drew into an alleyway, because it could make no possible difference to her whether Armand Laurent was married or not.

Gaby recognised the alleyway, even though it was as dark and gloomy as before, but this time as they passed beneath the archway she looked up and saw coloured murals in gilt-edged panels on the underside of the arch; delicate paintings of birds and animals, each in their own paradise of trees and flowers.

She held her breath in anticipation as Armand drove right into the courtyard. Things were so often never quite as glorious the second time, but as they passed from the darkness of the alley to the sudden brightness of the courtyard she wasn't disappointed.

Armand brought the car to a halt, switched off the engine and climbed out, then, coming round to the passenger side, he opened her door.

Slowly Gaby stepped out, then she stood for a moment simply absorbing the atmosphere.

It was as if time stood still in this secret place; not the slightest breeze stirred the leaves of the vine that climbed the balcony supports, or disturbed the bright geranium petals. The galleries were as silent as before, deep with shadows, their doors firmly closed, their windows shuttered.

'What is it?' Armand, sensing her mood, also lingered, one hand beneath her elbow.

'This place,' she murmured, glancing up—at the tower in the corner, at the profusion of flowers, and at a blue square of sky high above. 'It is so peaceful, so beautiful, so still.'

'Ah, you like the stillness?' he said softly.

She nodded, acutely aware of the touch of his fingers on her arm. 'Yes,' she said, 'I like the stillness. There is not enough stillness. People rush too much—they miss so much.'

'Do you encourage stillness in your counselling?' he asked.

Gaby paused, reflecting, then slowly she nodded and said, 'Yes, I suppose I do. Maybe I differ there from other therapists, I don't know. Many will advise activity—"Keep busy," they say. "Keep occupied at all costs," that sort of thing—but I sometimes think much more can be achieved by taking the time to be still, to observe, to listen. . .'

She turned her head as she spoke and realised that Armand was standing very close to her. She stiffened, waiting, expecting she knew not what. . . Then a shutter clicked on one of the balconies above them and the moment was gone, and Armand was moving her forward towards the dark green door.

The door closed behind them and Gaby was enveloped in the same evocative atmosphere as before—the dim light, the slivers of sunlight on the dark polished floor and the timeless feel of solid antique furniture. Today, however, there was no sign of the formidable Hélène, and the scent that had proved so elusive on the previous occasion had been replaced by a light, citrus fragrance that seemed to hang in the air.

The doors off the hallway were tightly closed, and Gaby wondered if they led to other apartments or whether the whole building belonged to Armand. She was about to ask him when he gestured towards the staircase and, side by side, they began to climb to the first floor.

When they reached the landing she expected him to open the door of the same room she had seen before; instead he led her further down the corridor and opened another door. He preceded her into the room, looking round as if he expected to find someone there, then stood back holding the door open and allowing her to enter.

The room was as charming as Gaby had come to expect everything about this house to be, with delicate, very French antique furniture and deep jewel-coloured furnishings in direct contrast with the plain ivory of the walls and paintwork. The shutters were closed, but again the sunlight intruded, edging its way to form patterns on the wooden floor and across the thick oriental rugs.

'Please,' said Armand, 'sit down. I will go and find Hélène, and I am sure you would like some refreshment.'

Gaby smiled at him and sat down in the corner of a vast sofa. There was something reminiscent of a bygone age about Armand's manners and charm, of an age of chivalry of which there was so little evidence in today's fast-paced world.

He was back almost immediately, accompanied by Hélène. Today, Gaby was able to study her a little more closely, and she quickly realised that the woman who looked after Armand was, in fact, older than she had at first thought. The dark hair drawn back into a severe pleat was streaked with silver, and the skin of her face and neck was criss-crossed with a fine network of lines. The plain but stylish grey suit she wore was topped by a fresh white blouse fastened with a tiny gold pin at the throat.

As Gaby stood up to greet her she got the distinct impression that the older woman wasn't enthralled at the prospect of giving her French lessons.

'I will leave you two to arrange suitable times while I make the tea,' said Armand.

Hélène turned sharply at his words, her gesture

indicating that she believed it should be herself preparing refreshments and not him.

Armand merely smiled, spoke in rapid French, glanced at Gaby, then added, 'Besides, the English love their tea.' As he disappeared out of the room Gaby turned apprehensively to Hélène.

'I hope you don't mind Armand arranging this,' she began.

Hélène gave a dismissive little gesture with her hands. 'Dr Laurent is my employer,' she said in heavily accented English, implying that that was the sole reason she was even entertaining the idea.

Gaby bit her lip. She had the uneasy feeling that this whole thing was going to be even more uncomfortable than she had feared. 'When would it be convenient for me to come here?' she asked after a moment.

Hélène shrugged. 'You work at the factory?'

'Yes.' Gaby nodded, then, thinking that Hélène might have the wrong impression, she added, 'At least, I see my patients there.'

'Your patients?' The woman frowned, the gesture throwing her features into sharp relief and making her face appear more forbidding than ever. 'You are a doctor?'

'No.' Gaby smiled in a desperate attempt to lighten the atmosphere, 'No, I am not a doctor,' she said. 'I am a counsellor.'

Hélène's frown deepened. 'What is this. . .counsellor? I do not know.'

'I try to help people cope with stress. . .with tension. . .' Gaby trailed off, aware that Hélène either did not know what she was talking about, or wasn't interested. She had an uneasy feeling that the latter was the case. 'Anyway,' she continued, 'I would be able to come here either late afternoon, evenings, or at weekends. Armand. . . Dr Laurent suggested at least twice a week.'

Hélène shrugged again, and as Gaby found h wishing that she could forget the whole thing, Ar returned with a full tea-tray.

He must have felt something of the tension

room, for he glanced quickly from one to the other. 'Have you arranged times?' he asked.

'One afternoon and one evening each week will suit us both,' Hélène answered rapidly in English, then added, 'Wednesday afternoons at four o'clock and Friday evenings at six.'

Her change of attitude, so obviously for Armand's benefit, almost took Gaby's breath away, and she found herself nodding numbly in agreement.

'How much French do you know, *madame*?' Hélène turned to Gaby.

'Oh. Only school French, really,' said Gaby. 'And a home-learning course that I started when I applied for this job.'

Hélène nodded. 'Just so I know where I need to start,' she murmured, then, turning to Armand, she said, 'If you will excuse me, I need to prepare for your next surgery.' Without so much as another glance in Gaby's direction she moved swiftly from the room.

'I'm sorry. I didn't know you had another surgery to do.' Gaby turned to Armand.

'Do not worry.' He shook his head. 'I have plenty of time. Here, drink your tea.' He handed her a delicate china cup and saucer. 'Then I will take you back to meet Monsieur Jackson.'

'Oh, yes.' With a guilty start Gaby took the cup and saucer and sat down again. She had quite forgotten Martin.

'You are not late,' said Armand as he swept into the factory car park. 'It is not quite five o'clock. You will not have kept him waiting. Does he take you home every night?' he asked after a moment.

'Yes, for the time being,' Gaby replied, then, when she saw his quizzical expression, she explained, 'I'm buying a car of my own—it's being delivered in the next day or so.'

Armand smiled his approval and she continued, 'Not that he's taking me straight home tonight.'

The minute she'd said it, she wished she hadn't.

'Oh?' Armand switched off the engine and turned

his head slightly, obviously waiting for an explanation.

She hesitated, then said, 'Martin has apparently found a property he wants to buy.'

'And?' He said it softly, so softly that she almost didn't catch the single word—the word that requested explanation.

'He wants me to go and see it,' she said.

'Ah, so he needs your approval?'

She shrugged.

'Do you know why?'

'What do you mean?' She threw him a quick glance, knowing exactly what he meant but playing for time.

'Why he should need your approval?' he said carefully, then, when she didn't answer, he went on, 'Maybe it's because he hopes you will be joining him there? That it will be your home also?'

Gaby did not answer, instead staring out of the car window at the tubs of flowers that edged the car park, realising that they were in fact geraniums, then marvelling at the variety of colours.

'Is that what he hopes, Gabrielle?' Armand murmured.

'Yes,' she said at last, and her voice came out as little more than a hoarse whisper. She cleared her throat. 'Yes, I suppose it is.'

'And is it what you want?' His voice had lost a little of its gentleness now, and had taken on a note of urgency. 'Is it?' he repeated.

'I. . .' She swallowed.

'Do you want to marry this man?'

'Marry?' She looked up, startled.

Armand shrugged. 'You seem surprised, but surely if he wants you to join him in this house he must mean marriage? Anything less would be an insult to you and to your son.'

As Gaby struggled to find a reply there came a sudden rap on the window. Startled, she looked up to find Martin bending down and looking into the car, glaring at them both.

CHAPTER SIX

'So YOU'VE been in Toulouse for nearly a year?' Gaby looked up from the folder on her desk to the young man sitting opposite her.

He nodded, and as he lifted one hand in a nervous gesture and gnawed at the side edge of his thumbnail she noticed that his fingers were stained with nicotine.

'I understand, Justin, from Sister Roberts,' she went on, 'that you have some problems at the moment.'

'Yeah, you could say that.' The young man folded his arms, thrust his long legs out in front of him and stared up at the ceiling.

He was quite handsome, really, Gaby thought as she watched him closely. His hair, thick and straight, was drawn back into a pony-tail and there was just enough stubble on his chin to give him an interesting look. But it was his eyes that drew one's attention—very dark, almost black, and with a glitter about them.

'Want to tell me?' asked Gaby suddenly, and Justin threw her a sharp look.

'What?' he asked, and there was suspicion in his tone.

'About your problems,' she replied patiently.

'Can't see what good that'll do,' he muttered.

'I can't solve your problems, Justin—' Gaby began.

'So what's the point in telling you?' he demanded, looking up sharply.

'Sometimes it helps just to talk things through,' she said, then, carrying on quickly, 'With someone who will listen—someone who is not involved.'

'Yeah, Sister Roberts said that,' said Justin, then, tightening his lips again, he added, 'I can't see it meself.'

'Why not, Justin?' asked Gaby.

'Well, stands to reason, doesn't it? You'll probably give me advice that I don't want to hear—'

'No,' Gaby interrupted, 'I won't. I told you—I'm here to listen, not to give advice, unless, of course, you ask me for my opinion. Even then it is only my opinion, and you don't have to agree.'

Justin frowned. 'I still don't see the point of it,' he muttered. 'I can't see how just talking about something can help anyone.'

Gaby sat back in her chair and stared thoughtfully at him, then, on impulse, she said, 'It helped me once.'

He threw her a quick, suspicious glance from beneath his dark eyebrows. 'What, talking?' he said, then, when she nodded in reply, he added, 'But you're different—you're into all this counselling lark, aren't you?'

'I wasn't then,' Gaby replied quietly. 'I've only been into it since I discovered what good it could do.' As she spoke she watched him closely, and saw by the flicker of his eyes that she had roused his interest. Not giving time for that interest to die, she went on quickly, 'I was once very depressed,' she said, 'totally unable to get on with my life or to come to terms with what had happened to me.'

'So what *had* happened to you?' He looked suspicious again, as if nothing that had ever happened to Gaby, or to anyone else for that matter, could possibly have any bearing on his own situation.

'My husband was killed in an accident,' she said quietly, 'leaving me with a young son.'

'Oh!' For one moment even Justin looked taken aback.

'It wasn't that I couldn't cope with everyday things,' Gaby went on after a moment.

'Then what. . .?' Justin's eyes narrowed.

'It was the nature of my husband's death I couldn't accept.'

'What do you mean?' He looked wary now, as if uncertain that *he* could cope with what she might be about to tell him. It was a look Gaby was well used to, had seen many times on the faces of others whenever Terry's death was discussed.

'He worked on an oil rig,' she said after a moment.

'There was a fire. He was trapped in a storeroom. He burned to death.'

'Jeez. . .' Justin drew in his breath sharply, then stared at her.

'For a long time I wasn't even able to think about his death, let alone discuss it,' said Gaby quietly. 'I shut it away in some dark corner of my mind, where it grew into some huge monster that threatened to devour me.'

'So what happened?' Justin looked quite stricken.

At that moment the intercom buzzer sounded on Gaby's desk. They both ignored it, and Gaby knew that she now had Justin's undivided attention. 'Someone suggested counselling,' she said. 'I was very reluctant at first. Like you, I couldn't see how it could work. But I was eventually persuaded to give it a try. It was the best decision I could have made.'

Justin was silent for a long moment, then he shifted restlessly in his chair. 'Yeah,' he said at last, 'maybe it worked for you. . .but with me it's different. My problem's nothing like yours. . .'

'But it's troubling you?'

'What d'you mean?'

'Whatever it is, *is* troubling you?'

'Yeah,' he admitted. 'Yeah, I s'pose it is.'

'It was troubling you enough to make you go and see Sister Roberts?'

He nodded.

'Why did you go to Sister Roberts, Justin?'

'I thought she might know someone who could help,' he muttered, without looking at her.

'Help you?'

He was silent again, and for one moment Gaby thought she had lost him. She was about to try a different tack when suddenly he sat upright in his chair.

'No,' he said, 'not me. Me girlfriend.'

'Your girlfriend?' Gaby threw him a quick glance.

'Yeah.' He inhaled deeply, and instinctively Gaby knew what was coming next. 'She's pregnant.'

'How far is she?'

He shrugged. 'Couple of months, I think.'

'How did you think Sister Roberts might be able to help?'

'I dunno, really.' He shrugged again. 'I thought she might be able to give me girlfriend something to take, or if not that she might know someone—you know. . .' He glanced at Gaby, then, in sudden desperation, he said, 'Well, it was an accident. We didn't mean it to happen.'

'So. . .' Gaby frowned. 'Did your girlfriend come here on holiday, or did this happen when you were on a trip home?' She spoke gently, but purposely kept her tone matter-of-fact. Justin, however, didn't answer, and when she looked up Gaby saw that he was frowning too.

'Justin. . .?' she prompted at last.

'You've got it all wrong,' he muttered. 'Me girlfriend lives here.'

'She lives with you?'

'No, she lives with her parents.'

'You mean they are employees of OBEX?'

'No.' Justin looked miserable now. 'She's a French girl. She's a waitress in her father's café, here in Toulouse—that's where I met her.'

Gaby took a deep breath. 'So how does she feel about this pregnancy?' she asked at last.

'She don't want it either.' Justin pulled a face. 'I told you—it were an accident. I thought she were on the Pill.'

'What you're saying is that neither of you wants this child, is that right?'

Justin nodded. 'Yeah, that's right. The problem is her parents. Her old man hit the roof. He says we should get married! Can you imagine it? Me, married?'

In spite of the seriousness of the situation Gaby felt her lips twitch. 'People do, you know, Justin,' she said at last.

'Yeah, I know,' he said, 'but not me. That's the last thing I want,' he muttered.

'So what do you think the solution is?'

'Well, it's obvious, isn't it?' He looked up sharply, and stared at her as if she was stupid.

'Not to me, it isn't.' Gaby shook her head.

'She has to get rid of it.'

'You believe that's the only option?'

'What else can she do?' He looked exasperated.

'So what about her parents? What would they think if she did that?'

He didn't answer immediately, continuing to gnaw the side of his thumb, then suddenly he said, 'They'll just have to get used to the idea. Won't they? Seems like they're against abortion—something to do with religion, I think—but they'll come round in the end.'

Gaby remained silent for a while, leaving Justin to his thoughts, then, after a while, she said, 'What's your girlfriend's name, Justin?'

'Eh?' He glanced up and stared blankly at her.

'Her name?' Gaby repeated quietly.

'Oh, Claudine,' he muttered. 'Claudine Flaubert.'

'Do you think Claudine might come and see me?'

'I dunno. I doubt it. Why?' He looked suspicious.

'I'd like to talk to her, that's all.'

'You want to speak to her on her own?' The suspicious look was still on his face, and Gaby knew that she would have to tread carefully if she wasn't to lose him completely.

'Not necessarily.' She shrugged. 'In fact it would probably be far better if she was to come with you. Do you think she would do that, Justin?'

'She might.' He looked doubtful. 'Why?' He hesitated. 'D'you reckon you might help us?'

'I don't know,' replied Gaby. 'What I do know,' she went on, seeing the flicker of disappointment that crossed his face, 'is that the answers to your problems lie within the two of you. Only you can discover them. Not me, or Claudine's parents, but you and Claudine. What I can do is to help you discover them.'

Justin didn't answer, just stared at the floor, then, when Gaby remained silent, he looked at his watch. 'I've got to go now,' he said, and stood up.

'Will you come again and bring Claudine?' asked Gaby. 'Perhaps in a few days' time?'

He hesitated, then nodded. 'Yeah, OK. I'll have to check and see when she's working.'

'Of course.' Gaby watched as he left the room, then, as the door closed behind him, she too stood up, stretching her neck muscles to relieve a build-up of tension. Crossing to the percolator, she poured herself a much needed coffee, then, curling her hands around the china mug, she turned and wandered to the window.

When she had first come to Toulouse she had been curious as to the nature of the counselling she would be called upon to give. She should have known really, she thought as she stared out across the pink city. As she'd said to Julie, peoples' problems were the same the world over, because even though cultures differed, and trends and fashions came and went, human nature didn't change.

At the sound of a light tap on her door she called out and turned from the window. The door opened, Armand appeared, and her heart skipped a beat.

'I come to see how you are,' he said. His English, as always, was impeccable, with just enough of an accent to make it sexily attractive.

'I'm fine,' Gaby replied lightly, desperately hoping that she gave nothing away even to suggest the effect he had on her.

'I was concerned.' Armand came right into the room and shut the door behind him. 'On Friday, when I left you in the car park, Monsieur Jackson did not seem too pleased.'

'Take no notice of Martin,' she said lightly. 'Would you like a coffee?'

Armand nodded and watched as she poured another mug of coffee. Then, as she handed it to him and sat down, he perched on the edge of her desk and stared down at her. 'But he was annoyed?' he said.

'Yes,' she admitted at last, 'he was annoyed. Or rather—' she considered for a moment '—more irritated than annoyed.'

'I'm not sure I understand why,' Armand said carefully. 'We were not late. He was not expecting to meet you until five o'clock. . .it was barely that. . .'

'I know. . .'

'Then what. . .?'

She looked up and found Armand watching her intently. 'I. . .I'm not sure, really,' she said. 'Martin's like that. . .he couldn't understand why we had been out together.'

'We are colleagues—is that not enough?' The surprise was only too obvious in Armand's voice.

'I suppose not.' Gaby swallowed and looked away. Suddenly she felt decidedly uncomfortable.

'So what else did he want to know?'

'Where we had been.'

Silence followed, then Armand leaned forward slightly, forcing Gaby to look at him again. 'Did you tell him?'

She nodded. 'Yes, I told him. Not immediately. But later I told him.'

'Why did you not tell him immediately?'

'He was in a hurry—we were going to see that farmhouse he's hoping to buy—and besides, I was angry with him for being so possessive.'

'Ah.' Armand moved back and sipped his coffee, then he said curiously, 'So what did you tell him in the end?'

'I told him we had gone to your house to talk to Hélène because you had kindly arranged for her to help me with my French. He couldn't say much, because he himself had suggested I do something about brushing up my French.'

'But he wasn't pleased.'

'Wasn't pleased? Well, I don't know. . .I think. . .'

Armand set his mug down and leaned forward again. 'He wasn't pleased,' he said again.

'No.' Gaby sighed. 'He wasn't pleased.'

'Tell me,' Armand said after a moment, 'about the farmhouse.'

Gaby shrugged. 'There's not a lot to tell.'

'Some of these old places are quite delightful and have much potential.'

'I agree.' Gaby nodded. 'And with time, money and

a little imagination I am sure the one we saw could be made absolutely charming.'

'But. . .?'

'But what?' She looked up at him, and for one moment thought she saw a gleam of amusement in his eyes.

'I thought I detected a "but" coming. . .'

Gaby gave a slight shrug and sipped her coffee.

'Where was it?' Armand was watching her closely.

'I'm not sure. . .somewhere near Fontaneille. It was quite isolated—in fact, there were no other houses for miles—and there were woods behind. . .a forest, really, a great black forest. I don't think Oliver would like it. . .'

'Did you tell Monsieur Jackson that?'

'Yes, I did.'

'And what was his reaction?'

'He didn't seem concerned. He said children soon adapt to new situations.'

'I see.' Armand paused, then quietly, deliberately, he said, 'So he has now asked you to marry him.' It was a statement rather than a question.

'No.' She corrected him quickly, then, seeing his raised eyebrows, hesitated before hurrying on. 'I'm not sure that was ever the intention.'

'Then what is?'

'That we simply live together and see where the relationship goes.'

'Would you say that Monsieur Jackson isn't the marrying kind?' asked Armand softly.

'I've no idea,' Gaby protested.

'He must be. . .what?. . .late thirties? Maybe he has been married before?'

'No. . .no, he hasn't. . .' She looked up swiftly, again saw the amusement in Armand's eyes, and, prompted by some sudden, impulsive urge, said, 'I could say the same about you. You must be in your mid-thirties. . .why aren't you married?'

He didn't answer immediately, continuing instead to stare at her in a faintly bemused fashion.

'But maybe you are?' she said softly, then found

herself holding her breath as she waited for his reply.

'No,' he said at last. 'No, I am not married.'

'Then maybe you also are not the marrying kind?'

'Oh, I am the marrying kind.' He said it softly, at the same time allowing his gaze to roam over her face and her hair, coming to rest, at last, on her mouth. 'Most definitely I am the marrying kind.'

'Then why. . .?'

'Have I never married?' He leaned forward again, until his face was only inches from her own. 'Because, Gabrielle, I had not found the woman I wanted to spend the rest of my life with.'

She found herself holding her breath again. His choice of tense had implied that now he had found that woman.

Giving her no time for further speculation, his lips touched hers in a kiss so gentle, so fleeting, that afterwards she was to wonder if she had imagined it.

He drew away almost immediately, but continued to watch her. 'Do you think you have found someone in Monsieur Jackson who you could spend the rest of your life with?' he said quietly.

'I don't know,' she whispered.

'Are you in love with him?'

'I. . .I thought I might be. He is the first man I've been attracted to since Terry. . .'

'He bears a strong resemblance to your late husband.'

She looked up sharply. So he had noticed. Her gaze flew to the photograph on her desk, then, when she looked up again, she saw that Armand was also looking at it.

'Yes,' she sighed. 'Martin does look like Terry.'

'Do you think that was what attracted you?'

'I suppose it might have been. . .at first.'

'And now that you know him better?'

'I've come to realise he is nothing like Terry,' she replied, surprised, as she said it, to experience a sense of shock. For while she might have acknowledged it subconsciously, it was another matter altogether to be putting it into words.

Armand stood up, then, leaning across the desk, he put one hand beneath her chin, gently tilting her face. 'Be careful, Gabrielle,' he murmured. 'Don't rush into something for the wrong reasons.'

She was prevented from answering by another knock on the door.

'Come in.' She answered without taking her gaze from his face then, as Armand straightened up, Mélisande came into the room.

'Your letters, Gaby. . .' The French girl trailed off as she caught sight of Armand, then her gaze flew back to Gaby. 'I'm sorry, I did not realise I was interrupting. . .in fact, I did not think you were here—you did not answer your intercom.' There was a faintly accusing note in her voice.

'I had a patient at that time,' Gaby replied, then, in a desperate effort to sound casual, she added, 'I'll sign the letters now—Dr Laurent is just leaving.'

Armand left the room, and while Gaby was signing the letters she was aware that Mélisande was watching her. At first she thought nothing of it, then, as the silence lengthened, she glanced at the French girl. Her face was set, her expression remote, and when Gaby handed back the sheaf of letters she barely acknowledged the fact, turning and leaving the room still in silence.

With a sigh Gaby sat down in her chair again and stared at the closed door. She had no idea what was wrong with Mélisande; if she'd done anything to upset her she was completely unaware of what it could be. In fact, when she thought about it, the last few days had all been something of a strain.

There had been her visit to Hélène, who had made it quite plain that she was only undertaking the tuition because her employer had requested it. That had been followed by Martin's moodiness on finding that she had been out with Armand, together with the visit to the farmhouse, which had been far from satisfactory.

Her conversation with Armand had raised even more questions in her mind about her relationship with Martin. Now, as her thoughts turned to Armand, she felt her heart jolt as she recalled that light touch of his lips on hers. It had been so gentle, so fleeting, it could hardly be called a kiss, but it had signified his concern for her. He had warned her to be careful, not to rush into a deeper relationship with Martin for the wrong reasons.

But what were her reasons?

Restlessly she stood up and turned once more to the window and the view she had come to love since coming to Toulouse. The sun was sinking, and the natural pink glow of the city was flushed to an even deeper tone. She, herself, had already suspected that she had first been attracted to Martin because of his resemblance to Terry—now Armand had made the same observation.

But was that all it was? Had her feelings not deepened, matured into anything else?

The realisation that they hadn't hit her like a shower of cold water.

She didn't love Martin. She never had. And a small, still voice deep inside told her that she never would.

It had taken Armand to make her face the facts. But where did she go from here? She had come to France, to a new job, bringing Oliver with her, to stay on a temporary basis with Penny and Tom—but the general assumption all round was that eventually she and Martin would get together.

When she had voiced her fears to her mother about the possibility of things not working out, her mother's response had been instantaneous—if that happened she was to return home.

It had been her let-out—a comforting thought. But now that she was faced with the reality was it what she wanted?

Home wouldn't be the same when her mother was married to Henry, kind as they both were, and difficulties would be sure to arise with them all living together.

And then there was her job. The position she had vacated at Branchester would have been filled by now, and besides, Gaby had always thought it a mistake to go back to a previous job.

But, quite aside from all that, she knew deep in her heart that she didn't want to go back. She liked living in France. She loved her job, and Oliver was happy. She was making friends—Penny, Tom, Adèle, Julie, Lisa—Armand. . .

Armand. Her thoughts halted, her pulse quickening as she thought of Armand. Was he anything to do with her wanting to stay in Toulouse?

Of course he wasn't, she told herself firmly. At least, no more than any of the others. She liked him being around, she couldn't deny that, and he certainly made her feel good with his slightly old-fashioned, romantic French charm. . .but that was definitely as far as it went.

Why, she hardly knew the man—hadn't even known he was single until a few minutes ago.

But it had pleased her, the fact that he wasn't married. Idly she wondered anew who the woman at his house had been that first day. Someone had been there with him; she had heard the laughter, caught the scent of her perfume. . . Abruptly she dismissed the thought—it was no concern of hers who Armand entertained at his home. . .

His home. . .that beautiful old house in the silent courtyard where she was to go twice a week for her French lessons. A stab of excitement hit her at the thought.

She mustn't think of that now. The most important thing was to see if she and Oliver could continue staying with Penny and Tom until she could find a place of her own.

But even before that—and her heart sank at the prospect—she knew that she had to talk to Martin.

CHAPTER SEVEN

THE following evening Gaby drove to Martin's lodgings in St Michel and told him gently but firmly that she had realised she didn't want their relationship to continue any further. Later, when she looked back on it, she came to the conclusion that he hadn't seemed too surprised, but at the time she was too apprehensive to notice.

'What will you do?' he asked, his back to her as he stared out of a window overlooking the deserted market square.

'What do you mean?' She was sitting at a scrubbed pine table, her elbows on its surface, her chin resting on her hands.

'Will you go home?' He half turned as he spoke.

'No,' she said quietly, and he turned fully then to look at her. 'At least,' she corrected herself, 'not immediately.'

'So what will you do?' he persisted.

'I'll stay for a while. I'll ask Penny if we can stay there for the time being. Later, I may look for a place of our own. I like Toulouse, Martin, and I love my job. . .the whole idea was that I gave it a good try.'

He gave a short laugh. 'I thought the whole idea was that we gave our relationship a good try. . .what about the farmhouse?'

She took a deep breath. 'I know, Martin, and I'm sorry—really I am. But nothing was ever really decided between us. And that's why I'm telling you now. I didn't want you to go rushing in and buying that farmhouse under false impressions.'

He shrugged. 'I'll probably buy it anyway—it's a damn good investment.'

'Well, that's up to you.' He'd turned back to the window and she stared at his back, amazed yet pleased that he seemed to be taking it so well. He remained silent for a long while, and she found herself thinking once again how unlike Terry he really was. At last, with a little sigh, she stood up.

'I'd better be going, Martin,' she said. 'Oliver will wonder where I've got to.'

'Are you sure you know what you're doing?' He turned again then, and stared at her.

'Yes.' She paused. 'I hope so. I really am sorry, Martin but I thought it best—'

'This is to do with that doctor, isn't it?' he said bluntly.

'Doctor?' She froze, then put one hand on the back of the chair.

'Yes—Laurent,' said Martin, and it sounded as if he spoke through gritted teeth. 'This is his doing, isn't it?'

Gaby stared at him in dismay and noticed that his face had flushed a dull red. 'Dr Laurent?' she said, trying desperately to stay calm. 'Why should you think it has anything to do with him?'

'He's turned your head with his fancy home and his smooth French ways. . .'

'No, Martin, he hasn't,' she said evenly. 'I have simply come to realise that what we had between us just isn't enough to be contemplating living together. I'm sorry, Martin, but I'm not in love with you.'

'I suppose you think you're in love with him? Well, be warned, love in this country has a completely different meaning. . .you mark my words!'

'I think I'd better go, Martin. I don't want to listen to this.' She began to move towards the door.

'You want to be careful—you need to watch yourself with the likes of him. He'll use you, then drop you. . .'

She didn't wait to hear more, hurrying out of the house to her car and, once inside, slamming the door and driving quickly away without a backward glance. She hadn't been under any illusion that it would be easy telling Martin, but on the other hand she had thought they might come out of it still being friends.

Now she wasn't so sure.

It was crazy of him to suggest that her decision had anything to do with Armand, but it was ironic that it had been Armand who had warned her against rushing into a permanent relationship with Martin if it might be for the wrong reasons, and now it was Martin who was warning her against Armand.

She had calmed down a little by the time she reached the Shackletons' house, but Penny immediately sensed that there was something wrong. The children were playing in the field by the stream with Adèle, and Penny brewed a pot of Earl Grey tea and carried it into the living room.

'Come and join me,' she said to Gaby. 'There are certain times when I think we need to revert to our English ways, and I sense that this is one of them.'

'You could well be right.' Gaby gave a deep sigh and sank down on the large, comfortable sofa.

'What's wrong?' Penny threw her a shrewd glance, the teapot poised in one hand.

'I need to ask a favour,' said Gaby.

'Fire away. If I can help, I will.'

'Thanks.' Gaby took the cup and saucer from Penny and placed it on a low table beside the sofa. 'I was wondering,' she said, 'whether Oliver and I can stay here for longer than we had originally intended.'

'Of course you can.' There was no hesitation on Penny's part. 'I told you when you came that you could stay for as long as it took.'

'I know you did, and I'm grateful, but it could be for quite a while.'

'Is there a problem?' Penny stared at her over the rim of her cup, her brown eyes full of concern.

'You could say that.' Gaby nodded, and for a moment found herself lost for words, totally unable to explain. In the end it was Penny who put the words into her mouth.

'Is it Martin?' she said quietly.

Gaby threw her a quick glance, then ruefully she nodded. 'Yes, it is,' she said, then, correcting herself, she went on, 'In actual fact, I suppose that isn't strictly true. It's me who's changed—not Martin.'

'So tell me what's happened.'

'Well, you know Martin was looking for a property to renovate?'

Penny nodded.

'The general idea was that when he did, and it was habitable, Oliver and I would move in with him.' Gaby took a deep breath. 'Well, he's found his farmhouse...and I've realised it's not what I want.'

Penny raised her eyebrows. 'The farmhouse, or living with Martin?'

'Both, I think.' Gaby took a sip of her tea. 'The farmhouse was only the shell of a building, really—oh, I know it could be made really nice,' she said, quickly catching sight of Penny's expression, 'but I knew I would never want to live there. Then I found myself questioning whether it was just that or whether I actually wanted to live with Martin...'

'And?'

'I realised I didn't.'

'Ah,' said Penny.

In the silence that followed the only sounds to be heard were the distant shouts of the children.

'Maybe,' said Gaby at last, 'I should have given the whole thing much more thought before I left England...I don't know.'

'I don't see why,' said Penny thoughtfully. 'The way I saw it was that you were seeing how things worked out. You've realised they are not going to work, and surely it's better that you've seen that now rather than after you'd moved in together? Think how traumatic that would have been for Oliver.' She paused for breath. 'Besides,' she continued, 'I don't see that your life depended on your relationship with Martin Jackson.' When Gaby didn't reply, Penny carried on. 'You like your job, don't you?'

Gaby nodded.

'Oliver is happy?'

'He seems to be.'

'And there's absolutely no reason why you shouldn't stay here for as long as you want.'

Gaby blinked as sudden tears threatened. 'You're a dear, Penny,' she gulped. 'I promise we won't take advantage. We'll start looking for a place of our own as soon as we can.'

'There's no hurry.' Penny set her cup and saucer down. 'Believe me, I'm glad of the company. It gets lonely here sometimes, especially evenings when Tom is late home.'

Gaby looked up quickly, puzzled by something in Penny's tone. 'I thought you went out a lot,' she said, 'parties and things.'

'I'm getting a bit tired of all the socialising,' said Penny.

'Is there anything wrong?' Gaby frowned, concerned now by Penny's manner.

'Tom and I aren't as close as we used to be.' Penny shrugged. 'We've been having a few problems just lately.'

'Do you want to talk about it?'

Penny appeared to hesitate, then said, 'That's not really fair, is it?' she said after a moment. 'You listen to other people's problems all day.'

'This is different.' Gaby was aware of growing concern. 'You are a friend, and you've been very good to me and Oliver. I'd like to help if I can.'

Penny was silent again, staring at the patterned rug on the polished wooden floor. When she finally looked up her eyes were suspiciously bright. 'I'm not really sure what's wrong,' she said. 'Tom has been very distant.' She absent-mindedly began plucking at a loose thread on the arm of the chair she was sitting in.

Gaby remained silent, knowing from experience that it was important to allow someone in Penny's position to get her thoughts into some sort of order.

'At first,' Penny went on at last, 'I thought it was just pressure of work. His job is very stressful.'

'I'm sure it is,' Gaby agreed. 'He has a very responsible position at OBEX.'

'I sometimes think he has too much responsibility,' said Penny. 'Not just for the job itself, but to the men under him—men who find themselves under stress simply through being in a different environment.'

'And to you,' remarked Gaby thoughtfully, and

when Penny looked blank she explained, 'He has a responsibility to you. . .and to the children.'

'Yes. . .yes.' Penny nodded in agreement, then, after a moment's thought, she said, 'I don't think we're very high on his list at the moment. In fact—' she took a deep breath '—If I'm honest. . .I think there's more to it. . .'

'What do you mean?' Gaby frowned.

'I think he's having an affair.'

'An affair? Tom?' Gaby stared at her, for one minute thinking that she was joking, then, when she realised she was serious, she said, 'Oh, surely not. . .he's too much of a family man, and surely that would only add to his stress.' She paused. 'Besides,' she added after a moment, 'he adores you, Penny. I'm certain of it.'

'That's what I thought. . .once. Now I'm not so sure.' Penny leaned forward, picked up the teapot, and as she began to top up her cup Gaby saw that her hand was shaking.

'What reasons do you have for thinking this?' Gaby asked after a moment.

'Nothing really specific.' Penny shook her head. 'Just intuition, really. I told you, he's become distant. . . he's gone off sex—which definitely isn't like Tom— and he's nearly always late home. . .'

'But any of those things could add up to overwork. . .stress of the job. . .'

'I know. . .but I can't help it. . . It's this feeling I have. . .I don't think he fancies me any more.'

'And you think he fancies someone else?'

Penny nodded, and looked so miserable that Gaby's heart went out to her. 'Do you have any idea who it might be?' she asked gently.

'Oh, yes!' There was no disguising the bitterness in Penny's tone, and Gaby stared at her in surprise. 'I know exactly who it is,' she went on, her fingers plucking even more furiously at the arm of the chair. 'His secretary, Mélisande Legrand—' She broke off sharply, her head jerking up as the door suddenly burst open and Sam hurtled into the room. 'Sam!' she exclaimed. 'I'm talking!'

'Harry fell in the stream!' Sam's face was red, his eyes bright with excitement.

'Oh, my God!' Penny leapt to her feet, and, closely followed by Gaby, hurried from the house.

They ran through the garden and were halfway across the field when they met the others—a subdued little group trailing through the poppies. A wet and bedraggled Harry, a superior and disgusted Charlotte, a calm, matter-of-fact Adèle and Oliver, who, together with Harry, was convulsed with giggles.

This is what he needs, thought Gaby, when she realised that no one had come to any harm, fun and adventure with other children.

And later, when she put him to bed, he told her, his eyes shining, 'I love it here, Mum.'

There was no further opportunity that evening for more talk with Penny, but what Gaby had learnt had given her much food for thought. There was no denying that Mélisande Legrande was an exceptionally attractive girl, but Gaby found it hard to believe that Tom Shackleton really was having an affair with her. She decided she would, however, keep a discreet eye on the situation while she was at OBEX, to see if she could disprove Penny's theory and at the same time put paid to her fears.

'I think,' said Hélène 'that is enough for one day.'

Gaby, her head reeling, was only too willing to agree, but in spite of all she had heard, and of Hélène's earlier reluctance, she was the first to admit that the older woman was an excellent teacher.

She was gathering up her books when Armand appeared in the doorway of Hélène's salon, where her first lesson had taken place. It was the first time she had seen him that day as it had not been one of his days for attending the factory, and she was aware of a quickening of her pulse.

'So how did it go?' He glanced from Gaby to Hélène.

Hélène inclined her head slightly. '*Madame* is an apt pupil,' she said. 'It makes all the difference.'

Gaby suspected that this was the nearest she would

get to praise, and gave Armand a rueful smile. He waited for her while she said goodbye to Hélène and confirmed her next lesson for Friday.

'Are you in a desperate hurry?' he asked as they began to descend the staircase.

'Not especially so.' She glanced at her watch. 'Penny knows I have a lesson—she is fetching Oliver from school.'

'Good. There is somewhere I would like to take you.'

'Really?' She threw him a quick glance, noticing how casual he looked in a rust-coloured polo shirt and cream trousers. 'Is it far?'

'No, not far.' He took her elbow as they reached the hall and guided her towards the front door. At the feel of his strong fingers Gaby felt her pulse race yet again.

The sun was still very warm as they crossed the courtyard, and Gaby paused and instinctively took a fringed cotton scarf from her bag. Without hesitation, Armand took it from her and placed it around her shoulders, lifting the mass of her hair as he did so. For one moment they stood very still in the silence of that secret place, Gaby hardly daring to breathe and Armand close behind her, so close that when he lifted her hair she felt his breath on the nape of her neck.

He didn't move immediately, instead, as he let her hair fall into place, lightly gripping her upper arms so that she, caught unawares, briefly rested against him.

It had rained earlier—a short, heavy shower that had done little more than wash away the dust of summer—and Gaby stood, mesmerised by the sight of raindrops trembling on the velvet surface of geranium petals.

It was a moment captured in time, and Gaby found herself wishing that it could last for ever. When at last she felt compelled to move, away from Armand, it was with a sigh, reluctant to break the spell. They passed into the cool darkness of the archway, he fell into step beside her, and she wondered if the moment had really been as intimate, as special, as she had thought or whether it had simply been a figment of her imagination.

Their footsteps rang out in the silence as they walked a maze of cobbled back streets, the tall houses on either side almost touching above their heads. An elderly man watched from an open doorway, his heavily lined face expressionless beneath his black beret, and two small children playing in the gutter looked up at them with solemn, dark eyes.

On leaving the narrowness of the back streets they passed through an arcade of pink-bricked alcoves housing shops packed with unusual glittering merchandise.

'This is where Lisa Rayner sells her jewellery.' Armand stopped before one of the shop windows. 'Did you know she made jewellery?'

'Yes, she told me.' Gaby gazed with interest at the beautiful pendants, earrings and brooches displayed on a backcloth of royal blue satin. 'She's very talented,' she said after a moment, her gaze coming to rest on a silver bangle set with aquamarine stones. 'Just look at the beauty in that piece.'

'Did she talk much to you?' asked Armand as they moved away from the shop.

'Yes,' Gaby replied, 'and I think we've got to the root of her problems.'

'Really?' There was no disguising the surprise in the single word.

'She's coming to see me again,' she went on quickly, 'but I think it's safe for me to say you won't be needing to prescribe many more anti-depressants.'

'You amaze me,' Armand replied. Gaby was only too aware of the trace of scepticism in his voice, and she knew she still had a long way to go before she could fully convince him of the benefits of her work.

They left the shopping arcade, following a pathway of the same rose-coloured bricks. On one side the walls of a church with a rounded brick tower soared above them and on the other steep banks formed a dry moat. Gaby was about to ask Armand if it had been Lisa's jewellery that he had wanted to show her when they began to descend a flight of steps which she realised led to the entrance to the church.

Armand paused and glanced at the sky, shielding his eyes from the sun with one hand. 'I think we may have timed this just right,' he said. Once again Gaby felt his hand beneath her elbow, and he guided her towards a pair of studded wooden doors.

The interior of the vast building was cool, the walls echoing with the whispers of centuries of prayer. The dozens of statues of the saints set in deep niches between soaring stained glass windows seemed content to keep the secrets of all they had seen during the passing of time, while the musky scent of incense hung in the air like some tangible thing.

It had just occurred to Gaby that the glass of each window was of a different colour when she felt Armand touch her shoulder.

'Look,' he breathed. 'Watch.'

She turned and saw that the window he was looking towards was of red glass, and even as they watched the sun must have moved, for its rays touched the glass, flooding the interior of the building with blood-red light. To those inside it was as if the building had caught fire, and there were gasps of amazement and murmurings of wonder from the groups of tourists.

'It's magnificent,' whispered Gaby, leaning against Armand as he slipped one arm around her shoulders.

They stayed until the sun moved, until it slipped below the red window, until the fire died and the interior was cool and dignified once more.

'That wasn't really what I brought you here for,' he said. 'That was. . .er. . .' He searched for the word he wanted.

'A bonus?' suggested Gaby.

'Ah, yes, a bonus. . .that is it. . .a bonus!' Armand laughed, as if the word amused him in some way, then he began walking towards the rear of the vast building.

Obediently Gaby followed him, quite happy to be in his company, to go where he went. She was aware that something was changing between them, that their relationship was entering some new dimension, but for the moment she was unwilling to analyse it. She had denied to Martin that there was anything between herself and the doctor, had convinced herself that she believed that...but...something was changing... She knew it, and she was certain that Armand knew it...

She followed him out of the building, passing beneath a stone archway into a corridor where, to her surprise, she heard the sound of a piano being played. She paused, in a sudden rush of pleasure recognising Rachmaninov—and Rachmaninov being played well. But there was no time for further speculation, for Armand, who by that time was a little distance ahead, had stopped, turned and was waiting for her.

As she walked towards him Gaby could tell by the expression on his face that he was waiting for her reaction to something—some thing or place that lay beyond him, some place as yet unknown, some place where Rachmaninov was being played...

She passed beneath yet another archway and joined Armand, then involuntarily she stopped. Before her the still, quiet garden, its low, maze-like hedges dotted with tall, slender conifers, was surrounded by cool shadowed cloisters, while directly above the mellow-bricked buildings of an ancient monastery slumbered gently in the afternoon sun.

'Le Cloître des Jacobins,' murmured Armand, taking her hand and drawing her forward.

This was another kind of peace—different from the fire and passion of only moments earlier, but equally as moving.

They walked the cloisters together, their footprints joining those on the worn flagstones of countless generations of holy men, pilgrims and tourists.

One section of the cloisters in the far corner held a small platform, and there they found the grand piano where a young woman, her blonde hair flowing around her shoulders, was bringing Rachmaninov's music to life.

Gaby listened, spellbound, and when the final notes echoed through the stone columns she joined in the enthusiastic applause of the few onlookers amongst the cloisters.

'Who is she?' she asked Armand as the young woman acknowledged the applause. 'Did you know she would be here?'

'Yes,' he admitted. 'I must confess, I did. Her name is Francine Galiana. She is a soloist with one of our finest orchestras. She is rehearsing for her forthcoming concert. I felt sure you would enjoy listening to her.'

'She is superb,' said Gaby wistfully. 'And you are clever, Armand, in knowing exactly what I would like.' She smiled up at him.

'It was not difficult,' Armand shrugged. 'Besides, you told me you love good music.'

That might be so, Gaby thought as a little later, reluctantly, while the strains of Debussy floated through the cloisters, she and Armand, still hand in hand, walked back through the church and into the street, but Martin would never have thought of it. Not in a million years would Martin have thought of it.

They walked back to Armand's house together, to Gaby's car which she had parked in the courtyard beside his black Italian sports car.

'Will you come inside again?' he asked as they lingered beside the cars. 'Perhaps a drink. . .?'

'No, really, I must go this time,' she protested. 'Oliver will be home by now. . .but thank you, Armand.'

He opened the car door for her, but before she could climb into her seat he caught her hand and she stopped. He was standing very close to her, so close that with every nerve in her body she was achingly aware of him.

'I think, Gabrielle,' he said softly, increasing the pressure slightly on her hand, 'I had little difficulty in knowing what would please you because my intuition told me. I think we have much in common.'

'I think you could be right,' she murmured. For one crazy moment she thought that he was going to kiss her; she even lifted her face in anticipation, felt the warm sun on her cheeks, would have closed her eyes in delicious expectancy. Then a movement in an upstairs window caught her attention. She glanced up and to her dismay saw a flash of emerald-green—the colour of the suit Hélène had been wearing. In that instant she knew the woman was standing there watching them, and the intimacy of the moment was gone.

'I'll see you tomorrow,' she said briskly, slipping behind the wheel and closing the door.

For one moment Armand looked bewildered—hurt, even—then he stood back as she started the engine. With a single wave of her hand she drew away, but a glance in her mirror revealed him standing there in the sunlit courtyard, watching her as she drove away.

CHAPTER EIGHT

SHE found Oliver with the Shackleton family in the garden. Penny was tending her window boxes, the children were sitting round the pine table beneath the loggia playing a board game and Adèle had just brought a tray of cool drinks from the house.

For once, Tom was there. Stripped to the waist, he was cutting the grass in the paddock behind the house. Gaby paused to watch him after parking her car, savouring the scent of the freshly mown grass and at the same time wondering anew about Penny's suspicions concerning Tom and his secretary. She had found herself watching Mélisande during the day, especially on the few occasions when Tom had been in the same vicinity, but there had been nothing even to suggest that there was anything to substantiate Penny's fears.

As if Tom sensed someone watching him he glanced up, and, because the sound of the motor mower rendered speech impossible, he raised one hand in greeting. She waved back, then as Oliver ran up to her she bent down to greet him.

It was really very pleasant, she thought a little later as she relaxed beneath the loggia with Penny, watching the children as they played their game. In fact, the day had really been quite special. . .or at least the latter part of it. . .Armand had acknowledged it by saying that he thought they had much in common, had proved it by pinpointing exactly what would please her.

'Mum?' It was Oliver who brought her back to earth with a jolt. 'Mum, is Martin coming tonight?'

'No, dear, not tonight.'

'Are we going to see him?'

'No.'

'Oh.' Oliver was silent for a moment, then he said, 'What about that house he wanted you to see?'

'I've seen it,' she replied.

'What was it like?' Oliver sounded wary, and Gaby realised that the other children had stopped their game and were listening with interest to their conversation.

'Well, it could most probably be made very nice,' she admitted.

'Will Oliver be going there to live?' asked Harry bluntly.

Silence followed his question—a silence in which everyone looked at Gaby. She took a deep breath. This was not how she had intended Oliver to find out that her relationship with Martin had ended. 'No, Harry,' she said at last 'Oliver and I are going to stay here for the time being.'

'Oh, brill!' said Oliver, and without asking more questions simply carried on with the game he was playing.

Gaby caught Penny's eye across the table just as Tom appeared by the loggia, wiping the sweat from his eyes with the back of his hand.

'This is thirsty work,' he gasped, then, eyeing the orange juice they were drinking, he said, 'Don't we have any beer?'

'I'll get you one.' Penny stood up, then disappeared inside the house while Tom picked up a T-shirt that was draped over one of the chairs. He was pulling it over his head when Gaby noticed a mark on his back that looked as if it had been bleeding. Thinking he had hurt himself whilst cutting the grass, she leaned forward for a closer look and saw that the mark was in fact a mole.

'Tom,' she said casually, and when he looked across to see what she wanted she went on in the same matter-of-fact tone, 'That mole on your back, does it hurt?'

'Eh? Mole? Which mole?' Tom paused, the T-shirt only half on, and craned his neck to look, but the mole was out of his vision.

'It's just here.' Gaby stood up, moved to where Tom was standing and lightly touched the area of skin alongside the mole. 'It looks as if it's been bleeding.'

'Oh, is that a mole?' Tom sounded vaguely

surprised. 'I hadn't realised that's what it was. It's been itching lately,' he explained. 'I guess I must have scratched it and made it bleed.'

'You're very fair-skinned, Tom,' said Gaby, 'just like me.' Then she added, 'Do you wear a sunblock?'

'No, he doesn't,' said Charlotte loftily, looking up from the game. 'We all do. Mummy says we must.'

'Mummy is quite right,' said Gaby. 'The sun's rays can burn skin very quickly.'

'I used to, when we first came out here,' said Tom with a shrug. 'But I have to admit, I don't bother these days,' he added.

'I think you ought to let Armand see that mole,' said Gaby.

'Armand?' Tom pulled his T-shirt down and looked at her in amazement. 'Oh, surely not. I can't bother Armand with something as trivial as that. He's a busy man.'

'That may be so,' Gaby persisted, 'but nevertheless I still think you should have a word. Armand is at the factory tomorrow. Why don't you slip into the centre?'

'I've got a heavy day tomorrow.' Tom frowned. 'We have a party of trade delegates arriving from Germany.'

'Even so. . .' Gaby trailed off as Penny appeared carrying a glass of beer.

She glanced from one to the other. 'Is something wrong?' she asked.

'Gaby's doing her nursey bit,' laughed Tom.

'"Nursey bit"? Whatever do you mean?' Penny looked puzzled.

'She says Daddy should go and see Dr Laurent,' said Charlotte. 'And I think he should go too,' she added primly.

'See Dr Laurent?' Penny looked bewildered, then threw Gaby a quick glance. 'What for?' She said it warily, almost as if she thought Gaby's suggestion might have something to do with her fears concerning Tom and his secretary.

'What I said,' said Gaby quickly, not wanting any misunderstanding, 'was that I thought Tom should let Armand see that mole on his back.'

'Mole? What mole?' Penny turned to her husband, who sighed, then lifted his shirt again so that she could see the offending mole.

'It's been bleeding,' said Charlotte.

'Daddy wasn't wearing sunblock,' breathed Sam.

'Do you think there could be something wrong?' Penny asked anxiously, after inspecting her husband's back.

'I don't know. I'm not sure,' replied Gaby. 'But it has been bleeding and Tom says it itches. I think it should be checked out. There's probably nothing wrong at all, but it's as well to be on the safe side.'

'Absolutely, Tom,' said Penny firmly. 'Go and see Armand tomorrow.'

'I think you're all making a fuss about nothing,' muttered Tom, taking a sip of his beer then wiping the foam from his upper lip. 'But I can see I'm hopelessly outnumbered.' He glanced round, then sighed. 'So I suppose I'd better do as I'm told.'

The following morning Gaby was in her consulting room waiting for her first patient, and as Lisa Rayner walked into the room with a jolt she realised that Armand was close behind her.

'Do you mind if I sit in on this session, Gabrielle?' he said, his eyes meeting hers.

Her gaze flew to Lisa's face as she wondered what her patient would think of the idea of having the doctor present.

'It is all right.' Armand must have anticipated her concern, for he intervened swiftly, giving her no time to voice her doubts. 'I want you to act as if I am not here. I have already spoken to Lisa, and she has no objections.'

Lisa nodded in agreement and sat down. She looked pretty that morning, in a floral dress and with her dark hair caught back with two jewelled combs. She also seemed less tense.

'Very well.' Gaby nodded, but she suddenly felt apprehensive. Armand was still sceptical of the work she did, and he had already indicated his disbelief of the progress she had made with Lisa. And, if all that wasn't enough, as Armand sat down in the corner of her room she realised that her heart, which had started to beat very fast from the moment he had walked into the room, was still behaving in a very erratic fashion. She knew it would be easier said than done to act as if he wasn't there.

They talked for a while of everyday things, then Gaby said, 'So tell me, Lisa, what's been happening to you since we last met?'

'Quite a lot, really,' Lisa said slowly.

'Do you want to tell me about it?' Gaby prompted.

'It was only after talking to you—' Lisa glanced up quickly '—that I realised I had never grieved properly for my mother.' She took a strand of her long dark hair and began twisting it between her finger and thumb.

'So how do you feel since you came to this conclusion?' Gaby, still acutely conscious of Armand's presence in the room, rested her elbows on her desk and propped her chin on the palms of her hands.

'Dreadful,' admitted Lisa.

'It had to get worse before it got better,' Gaby said gently.

Lisa nodded. 'I know that now.'

'It was all bottled up inside you,' Gaby went on after a moment. 'Your depression was a symptom.'

Lisa stared at the desk. Suddenly she looked up, directly at Gaby, and took a deep breath. 'I can see that now,' she said, 'but before nothing made sense.' She paused, as if wrestling with her emotions, then she began talking again, but so quickly that her words tumbled over each other in their hurry to get out.

'When I realised it all might be because of Mum's death, for the first time I allowed myself to think about her. Before that, if I found myself being reminded of her in any way—you know, a snatch of a song or a whiff of the perfume she used to wear—I would deliberately make myself think of something else. I thought by doing that, by getting on with my life— the life I have here in Toulouse with Charles—I could spare myself all that pain and grief. . .' Her words ended on a sob as she fell silent.

'So what do you do now, Lisa?' asked Gaby when the silence lengthened.

'I let the thoughts flood over me,' she said.

'And then?' prompted Gaby, when after another long silence it seemed as if Lisa might not say more.

'I cry,' she said simply, at last.

They sat in silence again, then Gaby said gently, 'And what about Charles? What does he do when you cry?'

'He holds me,' said Lisa. 'For hours, he just holds me.'

She fell silent again and Gaby watched her, watched the expressions that flitted across the girl's pretty, open features.

'You see—' Lisa looked up again sharply '—I feel so guilty when I think of Mum.'

'Do you know why you feel guilty?'

She nodded. 'Yes,' she said, 'because once we moved down here I didn't go home to see her as often as I should have done.'

'But you have your life with Charles,' said Gaby soothingly, 'and that is here, in Toulouse.'

'I know.' A frown creased Lisa's forehead. 'But even when I knew she was ill I didn't go as much as I could have done. It was because I didn't want to accept just how ill she really was.' She swallowed and began twisting her hair again. 'She had cancer,' she went on after a moment, 'breast cancer. . .I suppose I thought if I didn't have to see her like that, if I ignored the situation, it would go away and she would get better. And then. . .then when she didn't, I just couldn't bear it.' She shook her head in distress.

As the tears began to run, unchecked, down Lisa's cheeks Gaby heard a slight movement from the corner of the room, and with a jolt she realised that for a while she had actually forgotten that Armand was there. She was just wondering if she should bring the session to a close in view of Lisa's distress when the girl began speaking again.

'The funeral was horrendous. Like some sort of nightmare...I just wanted to get back here and get on with my life and pretend nothing had happened.'

'Only, of course, it had,' said Gaby quietly.

'Yes, it had...' Lisa trailed off and fell silent again, then quite suddenly she looked up and said, almost eagerly, 'Do you know what I did last night?' When Gaby raised her eyebrows, she rushed on, 'I took out the old photograph album—quite deliberately. I knew where it was, and I fetched it and looked through all the old photographs—the ones of Craig and me when we were children...with Mum and Dad...on holidays in North Wales...old photos of Mum when she was a girl...their wedding photograph...the one she and Dad had taken for their silver anniversary...'

'Tell me how you felt, looking at those photos,' said Gaby quietly.

'It hurt—it hurt terribly.' Tears shone again in Lisa's eyes as she spoke. 'But do you know,' she said, after a moment's reflection, 'the more I looked, somehow the easier it became, and afterwards I felt better... so much better...I can't explain.'

'I know what you mean,' said Gaby quietly, and when Lisa looked up in surprise she went on, 'Believe me, Lisa, the more you allow yourself to live with those happy memories of your mother, the easier the pain of losing her will be to bear. Now, tell me, how have you been sleeping?'

'A little better...'

'And eating?'

'Not really—not yet.' Lisa took a hankie from her bag and wiped her eyes.

'It's early days.' Gaby picked up her pen and jotted some notes on a pad in front of her, then, glancing at Armand, she said, 'I'm sure Dr Laurent will be wanting to see you again shortly to discuss your medication.'

Armand nodded and Lisa stood up. Turning to face him, she said, 'With a bit of luck maybe I'll soon be able to come off the tablets.'

'Yes,' Armand agreed. 'But not immediately, and not all at once—I shall want to wean you off slowly.'

'I see,' Lisa nodded, then looked at Gaby again. 'Will you want to see me again, Gaby?'

'Yes,' Gaby replied, then added, 'I should like you to come until you are fully off the tablets, and even after that if you feel you need someone to listen.'

'I'll feel that I'm wasting your time now that my problem has been identified,' Lisa protested.

'Not at all,' said Gaby briskly, standing up. 'Your problem may have been identified, and you may be well on the way to getting things under control, but it's been a very traumatic time for you and your emotions will feel bruised and raw for some time. In my book the antidote for that is to talk.'

'Well, if you're sure.' Lisa gave her a grateful smile, and with an uncertain glance towards Armand, who had also risen to his feet, she moved towards the door.

'I looked in the shop at your jewellery yesterday,' said Gaby as she moved round the desk and held the door open.

'Oh?' Lisa paused. 'Did you like what you saw?'

'Very much. I must pay you a visit some time—you have some beautiful pieces.'

As Lisa disappeared down the corridor Gaby closed the door. Suddenly she was apprehensive again. What would Armand's reaction be after sitting in on this session—and a session with one of his own patients at that?

'I am impressed,' he said softly as she turned to face him.

Gaby's breath caught in her throat, partly with relief, partly with pleasure. 'I've been relatively lucky with Lisa,' she said with a little shrug, in an attempt to sound casual and trying not to let him see her reaction. 'Her problem was fairly simple to identify. If only that was the case with all my patients.' She gave a rueful smile, then added quickly, 'There could, however, still be setbacks—even with what seems like a clear-cut case such as Lisa's. It can take much time and a great deal of patience to unravel some deep-seated traumas.'

'And that, of course, is where you have the advantage over us doctors.' He smiled and Gaby felt her pulse quicken, 'We,' he went on, his eyes not leaving her face, 'do not have the luxury of the time it takes to listen.'

'But you are recognising the need?' she asked lightly.

'From listening to you talk to Lisa—yes, I am beginning to see the benefits,' he admitted. 'Maybe, though, I am not yet totally convinced.' He paused, then, with a gleam of amusement entering his dark eyes, he added, 'Maybe what I need is to spend more time with you, so that you can carry on convincing me.'

'If you think that is necessary, Doctor,' she murmured, only too aware of the innuendo behind his words.

'Not only necessary, but essential.' He stood up and drew an envelope from his top pocket. 'And I suggest we make a start with this.' Opening the envelope, he drew out two pieces of paper and held them up. 'Saturday,' he said, 'Le Cloître des Jacobins—Francine Galiana in concert. Do you think that would be a good place to continue convincing me?'

'Oh, Armand—how wonderful!' She stared at him, so overcome that for the moment she was lost for words.

'I must go.' He smiled at her joy. 'Otherwise I shall be having to convince OBEX they still need to employ me. I shall see you at lunchtime—there is a meeting for the medical team.'

'Does that include me?'

'But of course—you are part of the medical team, Gabrielle, and, I am beginning to understand, a very important part.'

She could hardly believe Armand's apparent change of heart towards her work, and she was determined not to let anything happen to alter his newly formed opinion.

She saw two more patients that morning, both British employees of OBEX. One was a young man with serious alcohol-related problems and the other an administration officer who had just learnt that his wife, who had chosen to remain in England, had left him and moved in with his best friend.

By the time she arrived in the staff room at lunchtime she was feeling quite drained, but a smile from Armand quickly revived her flagging spirits, while crusty French bread, goat's cheese and a glass of red wine provided the required bodily sustenance before the real business of the meeting got under way.

The entire medical team was present: Armand, Julie, the unit's second nurse Suzanne, Luc the paramedic and Gaby. Mélisande Legrande was also there for the formal part of the meeting to take the minutes.

Julie Roberts, as the senior full-time member of staff, took the chair and declared the meeting open. Items on the agenda for discussion included staff rotas and hours, and medical cover for night shifts and unsociable hours which involved the factory's relief medical team.

Very few of these items applied to Gaby, and she found herself studying Mélisande. The secretary, looking chic in a black suit with a very short skirt and a scarlet blouse, was sitting slightly apart from the rest of them. Her long, slim legs were crossed and her shorthand notebook was resting on her knee as she took notes using a gold ballpoint pen.

It wasn't too difficult to see why any man would find her attractive, thought Gaby as Mélisande moved and she caught the evocative scent of the perfume she was wearing.

But an affair with a married man was another matter entirely...and with Tom Shackleton? Surely not... Oh, how she hoped not...

'What do you think, Gabrielle?'

She jumped and looked up sharply as Armand spoke her name. She had become so immersed in her thoughts that she'd completely lost track of the conversation.

'I'm sorry.' She raised her eyes to Armand's, becoming uncomfortably aware that the colour had flooded her cheeks as the others around the table waited for her reply. 'I didn't hear what you said,' she admitted.

The amusement in his eyes only added to her embarrassment, then, in an apparent attempt to spare her further humiliation, he said, 'We were wondering how you felt about more frequent staff meetings?'

'Oh. . .' She hesitated.

'You would object?' Armand raised his eyebrows. 'We were just discussing the merits.'

'Oh, I've nothing against them,' said Gaby quickly, 'provided they achieve something. From previous experience, I happen to think an awful lot of valuable consultation time can be lost in holding too many meetings, which in the end achieve very little.'

There were murmurings amongst the other members of staff, then Armand said, 'I am inclined to agree with Gabrielle.'

Gaby glanced up swiftly, and she was just in time to catch a strange, almost enigmatic expression on Mélisande's face before the French girl lowered her head again over her notebook.

The meeting wore on, then, when the administration business was over, Luc and Suzanne left to return to the treatment room and Mélisande went back to her office to type up her minutes, leaving the immediate medical team to discuss individual case histories.

'I understand Justin Metcalf has been to see you, Gaby,' said Julie, taking a folder from a stack in front of her and opening it.

'Yes.' Gaby nodded.

'He came to me,' said Julie. 'I think he thought I could arrange a termination for his girlfriend.'

'Who is his girlfriend?' asked Armand.

'A local girl, Claudine Flaubert,' replied Julie. 'She works as a waitress in her father's café in La Rue des Fleurs.'

'I know the Flaubert family,' said Armand slowly. 'Do they know Claudine is pregnant?' He looked at Gaby.

'They do,' she said. 'Apparently they are very unhappy.'

'Yes, they would be. . .' said Armand. 'And Claudine,' he added, 'you say she wants a termination?'

'According to Justin, she does.'

'I would not count on it,' said Armand.

'Well, I hope she'll be coming to see me...with Justin,' said Gaby. 'That is what I have suggested.'

'What advice will you give?' Julie looked curious now.

'I don't give advice,' replied Gaby quietly. 'I will encourage both of them to talk it through and decide for themselves what it is they really want.'

'I can't see Justin wanting to settle down,' observed Julie. 'He's a bit of a tearaway.'

'Maybe.' Gaby shrugged. 'It doesn't alter the fact that he now has a responsibility to face up to. Whatever course of action they decide upon, I hope I'll be able to make them see that. If I don't, then I fail in my job.'

'Did they take precautions?' asked Julie.

'Justin apparently assumed Claudine was on the Pill.'

'And Claudine obviously wasn't. . .' Armand drew in his breath. 'Well, Gabrielle,' he said, 'keep us informed. What else do we have?' He turned to Julie.

Julie looked at her folders again. 'Keith Bryony has been to see you too, Gaby?'

'Yes, I saw him this morning.'

'Bryony?' said Armand. 'I don't think I know him.'

'He's in administration,' replied Julie. 'He has just learnt that his wife has left him and gone off with his best friend.'

'Is the wife here in Toulouse?' asked Armand.

Gaby shook her head. 'No, she's in England. According to Keith, she had wanted him to take a post in Branchester. But he saw that as a sideways step in his career, and when the Toulouse posting came up he took that instead.'

'How is he taking the news about his wife?'

'He seemed stunned. Devastated, really,' said Gaby. 'Apparently she's taken the two children with her.'

'And the other man involved? You say he is Keith's best friend?'

'Yes, they were at school together.'

'Does he work for OBEX?'

'Yes.' Gaby nodded. 'He's at the Branchester factory. I thought I might contact Rachel Markham, the sister in charge of the medical team in Branchester—with Keith's consent, of course—just to put them in the picture.'

'Any other recommendations?' asked Armand.

'Possibly something to help him sleep—but that's your department, Armand.' Gaby paused. 'Apart from that, I think what is needed is a spell of leave for Keith, so that he can go back to England and try to sort out his domestic problems.'

'I agree,' said Julie. 'It isn't easy being separated from your family. I really feel for Keith—just as I do for Justin. . . It isn't easy having a relationship with someone from a different background either.'

'Ah, you would know about that.' Armand smiled. 'So how is your romance, Sister Roberts?'

'My romance is fine, just fine.' Julie grinned. 'All I'm saying is, it isn't always easy.'

'I'll have a word with Tom Shackleton about Keith Bryony,' said Armand. 'I agree he should go home.'

At his mention of Tom, Gaby looked up. 'Did Tom Shackleton come to surgery this morning, Armand?' she said.

'Tom?' He frowned. 'No.'

'Oh, dear. And you don't have another surgery until Monday, do you?'

'No.' Armand shook his head. 'Why? What is this? Is there something wrong with Tom Shackleton?'

'I'm not sure,' said Gaby. 'I hope not,' she added as Armand and Julie both stared at her. 'I told him he had to see you today,' she said to Armand, 'to show you a mole on his back. I noticed it when he was working in the garden without his shirt. It was very dark, it had been bleeding and the edges looked ragged. When I mentioned it to Tom, he said it had been itching.'

'I hope he was wearing sunblock, working in the sun like that,' said Julie.

'I asked him that,' said Gaby, 'and he said no.'

'Oh, for goodness' sake!' Julie exploded. 'How many times have I told them all? The sun here can get really lethal at times.'

'I know.' Gaby pulled a face. 'Tom said he used to use sunblock when he first came here, but that he hasn't bothered lately.'

'I can see we shall have to have a few staff pep talks,' said Julie grimly.

'Yes, and I think you could include some warnings about the availability of cheap alcohol in those,' said Gaby, 'because that's another problem that seems to be cropping up frequently.'

Armand glanced at his watch, then stood up. 'I'll go and find Tom now,' he said.

'Armand?' Gaby hesitated as he turned and looked at her, then said, 'Is it all right if I bring Oliver with me to my lesson tomorrow?'

'Of course it is,' he said.

'Penny has been invited out with her children and Adèle is having the day off.'

'I told you before—you can bring him with you whenever you like.'

She and Julie watched as Armand left the room, then Julie said, 'What was all that about?'

'Armand's housekeeper, Hélène, is giving me French lessons.'

'Oh, I see—you said before that you wanted lessons.' Julie stood up and stretched. 'I'd better get on.' She sighed. 'I have a blood pressure clinic this afternoon.' She paused. 'I hope poor old Keith sorts himself out. I like him. I'd hate to see his marriage break up. He thinks the world of his kids. Still, these things happen—not a lot we can do, really. . .'

Gaby stared thoughtfully at her, then on a sudden impulse she said, 'Talking of these things—and strictly between ourselves, Julie—you don't think there's anything like that going on with Tom Shackleton, do you?'

'Tom?' Julie turned and looked at her in amazement.

Gaby nodded.

'Well, I wouldn't have thought so,' Julie said. 'He's so much the family man—and he and Penny. . .' She left the sentence unfinished, then her eyes narrowed and she said, 'What makes you ask?'

'Nothing, really.' Gaby shrugged. 'I just wondered.'

She glanced at Julie and saw by her expression that she wouldn't be content with that. 'It was a chance remark someone made, that's all—a remark about... about Tom,' she went on, not wanting to say that it was Penny who had told her. 'Tom...and...and... Mélisande Legrande.'

'Mélisande?' Julie stared at her, then she gave a short laugh. 'Well, if Tom is carrying on with someone, which I very much doubt, it certainly isn't with Mélisande—I can assure you of that!'

'Oh?' Gaby raised her eyebrows.

'Yes.' Julie hesitated, then said, 'I'm not really supposed to say, but what I *can* tell you is that Mélisande *is* very much involved with someone—.' At that moment the phone rang and Julie turned to answer it. 'Hello?' she said into the receiver, and then while the caller spoke she mouthed to Gaby, 'And it's not Tom Shackleton.'

Gaby smiled in relief and, leaving Julie on the phone, left the staff room and made her way back to her consulting room.

'You must think me incredibly stupid.' Helplessly Gaby shook her head and closed her book. 'I never could master French verbs when I was at school either.'

Hélène inclined her head slightly but made no comment. The lesson had been tough, with the Frenchwoman making no allowances. Gaby was relieved that it was over.

'I'd better go and find Oliver,' she said.

When she had arrived she had settled Oliver in a corner of Hélène's room with his book and colouring pens, but within minutes Armand had appeared and whisked him away. Now, as Hélène followed her to the door, it was suddenly flung open and Oliver stood there beaming while behind him Armand was looking boyishly sheepish.

'I've had a brill time, Mum!' Oliver said. 'Dr Laurent's been showing me his soldiers. We've been playing battles.'

'Soldiers?' Gaby raised her eyebrows.

Armand grinned. 'War games. I have a collection. I think Oliver has just learnt an alternative version of the Battle of Waterloo.'

Gaby smiled. 'Well, it's kind of you to entertain him.'

'I said I would.' Armand looked happy and relaxed. 'Besides,' he went on, 'I enjoyed it—and I knew Oliver would. My nephews like to play with the soldiers when they come here.'

'Can I play with them again another day?' asked Oliver eagerly.

'Of course you can,' said Armand. 'You can come with your mother whenever you like, and if I am not here you know where the soldiers are.'

Oliver beamed again, and not for the first time Gaby thought how happy he now seemed with his new life and the friends he had made. Neither had there been any recurrence of his asthma since that day—the day when Armand had come into their lives.

Glancing up, she found Hélène watching them, her expression inscrutable, and momentarily Gaby's sudden feeling of happiness was replaced by one of unease, even though she was at a loss to explain why.

'We must be going, Oliver,' she said. 'It's past your bedtime.'

'I'll see you to your car,' said Armand.

They were barely halfway down the staircase when Armand said, 'I'll pick you up about seven tomorrow evening.'

'Where are you going?' Oliver, who was in front, turned and looked at them.

'To a concert,' Gaby explained, and at the same moment heard a door close on the landing above them. When she glanced up she realised that Hélène had gone back into her room and shut the door. Gaby sighed and continued on down the stairs. Once or twice she had thought she had started to break through the Frenchwoman's reserve, but at other times she'd wondered if she ever would. She knew, however, that she mustn't let Hélène's apparent coldness get to her. If the woman didn't want to be friends there was very little she could do about it.

'You don't mind if your mother comes to this concert with me?' said Armand to Oliver as they walked out of the house into the courtyard.

''Course not,' said Oliver, opening the car door and scrambling inside. 'Anyway, concerts are boring.'

Gaby smiled, and was about to get into the car herself when she stopped and looked back at Armand.

'Did you see Tom Shackleton?' She spoke quietly, so that Oliver couldn't hear.

'Yes.' Armand nodded, then said, 'My fears are the same as yours.'

Gaby stared at him in dismay.

'I've arranged for him to go to the hospital for excision on Monday.'

'How did he take it?' she asked softly.

'I don't think he is aware of the possible seriousness of the situation,' said Armand, his mouth tightening. 'But then people rarely are. We can only hope we have caught it in time.'

'Thank you for telling me,' said Gaby, getting into the car. As Armand closed her door she wound down the window. 'At least I'm prepared now for any reaction from the Shackletons.'

'They have you to thank for discovering it,' Armand said, then, his tone softening even more, he added, 'I will see you tomorrow at seven.'

'Yes.' Her eyes met his and her heart skipped a beat. There was something there in his expression that she found difficult to define. A promise of something—but of what, she couldn't be sure. She only knew that she was looking forward to going to the concert with him more than anything she had looked forward to for a very long time.

'I really like Dr Laurent,' said Oliver as they drove away, then, when Gaby didn't answer because she was so overwhelmed by her own feelings, he said anxiously, 'You like him too, don't you, Mum?'

Gaby took a deep breath. 'Yes, darling, I do,' she replied. 'He's a very kind man.'

'Mum?'

'Yes, Oliver?' She glanced at him in her rear-view mirror.

'Don't call me darling,' he said seriously. 'Harry says it's cissy.'

'All right, da—Oliver. I'll try and remember.' She smiled and drew out onto the dual carriageway, following the signs for St Michel.

CHAPTER NINE

AFTER Oliver had gone to bed Gaby went in search of Penny. She found her outside in the balmy warmth of the May evening, sitting at the table beneath the loggia writing letters. She looked up as Gaby approached.

'Hello,' she said, 'come and join me.'

'I'm interrupting—you're busy,' said Gaby.

'No, really—I'd almost finished anyway.' Penny replaced the cap on her pen. 'I was just catching up on letters home. Some people I phone these days, but my parents still like a letter, and so do one or two elderly relatives.'

'I don't think a phone call could ever take the place of a letter,' said Gaby, sitting down.

'So how has your day been?' Penny moved her own chair so that they could both sit and look out across the poppyfield.

'Pretty good actually.' Gaby nodded. 'I really feel I'm getting to grips with the job now.'

'And what about your French lessons—are you getting to grips with those?' Penny threw her a sidelong glance.

'Well, I'm trying.' Gaby pulled a face. 'But I'm sure Hélène thinks I'm really thick.'

'I shouldn't think she thinks that for one moment,' said Penny briskly.

Gaby shrugged. 'Maybe not, but it doesn't alter the fact that she doesn't really want to teach me. I'm convinced she's only doing it to please Armand because he happens to be her employer.'

'And Armand's only asked her to please you. . .'

'Oh, I don't know about that,' said Gaby quickly. 'He's done it to help me, certainly, but. . .' She trailed off, leaving the sentence unfinished, then after a moment she said, 'Speaking of Armand, he's asked me to go to a concert with him tomorrow night.'

'A concert?' Penny raised her eyebrows.

'Yes, it's in an old monastery. I can't remember the name of the place—it's a church. . .and there are cloisters.'

'Oh, you mean the Jacobins,' said Penny. 'Someone once told me they have recitals there, although I haven't been to one personally.'

'I would really love to go—I so miss my music,' said Gaby passionately. 'I go to concerts whenever I can at home. . .and if the pianist I heard rehearsing is anything to go by it will be a wonderful performance.'

'You've been there?' Penny looked surprised.

'Yes.' Gaby paused, wishing she hadn't said that, for Penny's expression indicated that she wanted to know more. 'Armand took me there after the first lesson at his house. . .' she added weakly.

'Really?' Again Penny raised her eyebrows, and Gaby felt the colour touch her cheeks. Not giving Penny a chance to comment further, she rushed on, 'Do you think Adèle would listen for Oliver for me?'

'I'm sure she would,' Penny paused then said, 'Tomorrow night, you say?'

'Yes. . .'

'Well, if Adèle can't, I shall be here. . .' She sighed. 'Tom will probably be late again.'

'Surely not on a Saturday night?'

'It doesn't seem to make any difference what night it is. I told him this morning he might as well move in at OBEX, he spends most of his time there anyway—or so he says,' she added bitterly.

Gaby hesitated, uncertain that this was the right time to repeat what Julie Roberts had told her, then, glancing at Penny again, and seeing the misery in her eyes, she came to a rapid decision. 'Penny,' she said, 'talking of Tom. . .'

'Yes?' Penny looked up sharply.

'About what you were telling me. . .' said Gaby.

Penny stared at her. 'You've found something out, 'en't you?' Her voice was flat, almost devoid of
 ˙n.

'No,' said Gaby quickly. 'Quite the opposite, in fact. . .Well,' she corrected herself, 'I didn't actually hear anything about Tom, but I did hear, from a reliable source, that Mélisande Legrande is very much involved elsewhere.'

Penny continued to stare at her, and Gaby couldn't fail to notice the sudden relief in her eyes. 'With someone else?' she said at last.

'Yes.' Gaby nodded, emphasising the fact.

Penny was silent for a moment, as if wrestling with her thoughts, then slowly she said, 'Maybe I was wrong. Maybe he isn't having an affair—but if he isn't, how do you explain everything? The late nights, the remoteness, the going off sex? Or maybe it was Mélisande I was wrong about. Maybe it isn't her he's having the affair with. . .Maybe it's someone else. . .' Helplessly she shrugged and trailed off.

'I don't know why you think it has to be an affair at all,' said Gaby. 'All those things you describe could simply be symptoms of stress caused by overwork.'

'Or worry,' said Penny quietly.

'Yes, or worry,' agreed Gaby, then, thowing Penny a quick glance, she said, 'Anything in particular in mind?'

Penny didn't answer immediately, and in the quietness all that could be heard was the singing of crickets from the long grass and the distant croak of a frog near the stream. 'This mole on his back,' she said slowly at last. 'Could he have been worrying about that?'

'It's possible,' Gaby replied carefully. 'Although when I pointed it out to him, he said that apart from the itching he hadn't been aware of it.'

'Did you know he has to go to the hospital on Monday to have it removed?' asked Penny after a moment.

Gaby nodded. 'Yes, Armand did mention it.'

There was another silence, then Penny said, 'How serious is it, Gaby?'

She swallowed. 'Well, I don't really—' she began, but Penny cut her short.

'Yes, you do,' she said swiftly. 'You're a nurse. You know exactly.' Then, when Gaby remained silent, she went on, 'Come on, Gaby, give it to me straight. I want to know.'

Gaby took a deep breath, then said, 'What Tom has is a melanoma. To all intents and purposes it is benign—but it has changed colour, it has been bleeding and itching, and the edges of it appear ragged. Because of these things it is better that the melanoma is removed.'

'Has it been aggravated by the sun?' asked Penny.

'Probably.' Gaby nodded. 'Tom is very fair-skinned...like me. We do tend to be at risk more than most, although it is becoming more and more evident, with all this talk of the hole in the ozone layer, that everyone should be aware of the dangers from the sun's rays.'

'So what happens after the mole has been removed?' Penny threw her a sidelong glance. 'Is that an end to the matter?'

Gaby hesitated for only a moment, then replied, 'Hopefully...yes.'

'What do you mean..."hopefully"?' asked Penny sharply, then, before Gaby had the chance to answer, she went on, 'You're saying it could be cancerous, aren't you? Aren't you, Gaby?' Her voice rose slightly.

'Yes.' Gaby nodded. 'It could be malignant. But we won't know for sure until after it's been removed.'

'Oh, my God!' muttered Penny. 'I can't believe this is happening. This is the sort of thing that happens to other people, not to us...'

'Penny—' Gaby turned and placed one hand reassuringly on her friend's arm '—please don't upset yourself...I'm sure everything will be all right once it has been removed.'

'You said *hopefully* it would be all right. What exactly did you mean by that?'

'Well, even if it does prove to be malignant, and they remove all the cancerous cells, then that will be an end to it.'

'I see,' said Penny quietly. The crickets stopped singing, and in the sudden silence she said, 'And what if they don't? What if they can't remove all those cells...what then?' She turned to look at Gaby, and Gaby saw the unmistakable dread in her eyes.

'Then he will be given some radiation to get rid of the remaining cells,' said Gaby firmly. 'But it may not come to that. You have to think positively, Penny, and you have to be there for Tom and help him through this.'

As they sat in silence two ducks rose from the stream and flew sedately across the poppyfield. Gaby was just thinking how cruel life could sometimes be, when Penny gave a sigh. 'You're absolutely right,' she said at last. 'Tom needs me now like he's never needed me before—whether he's having an affair or not.' She stood up. 'I heard his car just now. I think I'll go and find him. Do you mind?'

'Of course not.' Gaby smiled. 'You go.'

She continued to sit there alone after Penny had gone, watching the sky deepen from rose to crimson and the daylight turn to dusk. She desperately hoped that all would be well with Tom and knew that there was every chance it would be...provided the melanoma, if it proved to be malignant, had been caught in time.

Eventually, as the darkness crept into every corner, she too stood up and turned to go into the house. Tomorrow was Saturday. A thrill shot through her at the thought. Tomorrow Armand was taking her to a concert.

A mist hung over the fields the following morning, shrouding the trees and bushes with its eerie presence, silencing even the call of the cuckoo. But by the time Gaby left the house with Oliver and Harry to walk to St Michel the sun was struggling through, its warmth only a promise of the heat to come.

They spent a couple of hours wandering through the market stalls, talking to the friendly stallholders and practising their French. Gaby bought fruit and bread and a new pair of jeans for Oliver. The two boys spent their pocket money, then, as the clock in the church belfry struck eleven, Gaby took them to one of St Michel's two street cafés and they sat beneath a striped umbrella, drank lemonade and ate glazed apple pastries topped with almonds.

Later, on their return to the house, the family gathered beneath the loggia for lunch. Gaby was pleased to see that Tom was there, and thought that she detected a different atmosphere between him and Penny—one of forced gaiety, perhaps for the sake of the children, but at the same time reinforced by a quiet acceptance and a sense of unity. Whatever had to be faced, they would do so together.

The day was pleasant, but throughout it Gaby was aware of a growing feeling of excitement as the evening grew nearer.

And later, after a leisurely soak in a scented bath, she found herself dressing with great care, choosing a layered dress of delicate chiffon with a multi-coloured pattern in muted shades of cornflower-blue and lilac. Her hair she wore loose, brushing it out so that it framed her face in a soft cloud, and her only adornment was a long chiffon scarf that matched her dress and which she tied around her throat.

As she gazed at her image in the bedroom mirror she knew instinctively that Armand would approve, because even in the short time she had known him already she was very much aware of his likes and dislikes. Martin would not have noticed what she wore—even if she'd changed her dress three times in a single day he would not have noticed. Terry, yes—but not Martin. . . And now Armand. . .

He would notice, and he would approve. . .

After adding a light mist of her favourite perfume to throat and wrists she was ready, but when she turned to leave the bedroom she found Oliver standing in the open doorway, watching her.

'You're going to that concert,' he said.

'Yes, darling. . .sorry—Oliver,' she corrected herself. 'Adèle is going to look after you.'

Oliver shook his head. 'No, she isn't. Harry's mum has given her the night off. They aren't going out tonight. They've asked me to play games with them—they've got Scrabble and a Power Rangers game and—' He broke off, and suddenly, suspiciously, he said, 'Will you be going out with Martin again?'

'No.' Gaby shook her head, then, realising that this could be the right time to talk to him, she took a deep breath, 'No, Oliver, I shouldn't think so. It wasn't really going to work out with Martin and me. . .'

'Now you're going out with Dr Laurent?' He said it casually but Gaby threw him a quick glance, not wanting him to think that she was being fickle, but not knowing quite how to explain.

'Yes, dear,' she said. 'Does that bother you?'

''Course not. . .I told you, I like Dr Laurent.'

'Didn't you like Martin?'

'He was all right.' Oliver wrinkled his nose. 'But. . .' He slipped off the bed and, leaving the sentence unfinished, ran off along the landing then clattered down the stairs to join the others.

'So Oliver considers I am a suitable escort for his mother?' Armand smiled across the table, his head tilted slightly, his features thrown into sharp relief in the light from the single candle as Gaby finished recounting the story to him.

'He must do.' Gaby, still intoxicated by the music they had just listened to, laughed. 'He was nowhere to be seen when I left the house.' She glanced around her with interest. The peace of the cloisters had been replaced by the atmosphere of a busy, yet intimate restaurant.

'And there's been no sign of his asthma since that attack?' asked Armand thoughtfully. Raising his glass, he stared critically at the rich red wine he had chosen.

Gaby shook her head. 'I'm beginning to think,' she said, 'that it may not have been triggered by pollution or the weather after all.'

'Are you thinking it could have been stress-related?'

'I suppose it could,' she said slowly, then, when

Armand remained silent, she went on, 'Thinking about it, it must have been stressful for Oliver—coming to a new country, having to make new friends, leaving his old ones behind...not to mention his grandma... and the prospect of starting a new school.'

'That conjures up the overall picture, certainly,' said Armand, pronouncing his words with care. 'But can you recall exactly what happened immediately prior to the attack?'

Gaby frowned, considering. A waiter brought a basket of bread and a platter of pâté de foie gras to their table, placing them between the carafe of red wine and the green bottle that held the candle. Armand ordered the main course, and after the waiter had moved away she said, 'We were with Martin, of course, but you already know that...We had been to a café...then we went to some shops to buy postcards to send home. It was after that, after we'd left the shops, that Oliver began to cough.'

'Did anything happen in the shops to cause him anxiety?'

'I don't think so...' Gaby shook her head, frowning as she tried to recall.

'And at the café? What about at the café?'

'No, nothing...we were simply talking, that's all.'

'Can you remember what about?' Armand leaned forward slightly.

'Only general things.' Gaby shrugged, at the same time thinking how casually handsome he looked in his tan-coloured jacket and polo-necked shirt. 'Nothing to upset Oliver,' she went on hastily, when it seemed as if Armand might be about to ask what she was looking at. 'Martin was asking if we were comfortable at Penny and Tom's house...'

'Which you are,' said Armand quietly.

'Oh, yes—yes we are,' she agreed quickly. 'Then he went on to say that he too wanted to buy an old property and renovate it...But again, nothing that could have upset Oliver.'

'Hmm.' Armand helped himself to pâté, spreading it onto a piece of bread, then, after a moment, he said, 'Don't you think Oliver likes Monsieur Jackson?'

'I'm beginning to wonder,' said Gaby. Then she sighed, 'I thought he did... At least he seemed to, when we were in England...'

'But now?' prompted Armand.

'Now I'm not so sure,' admitted Gaby.

They remained silent for a while amidst the murmurings of the other diners.

The restaurant was on the ground floor of a tall, typically French house of grey stucco, with shuttered doors that opened directly onto the pavement. The tables were concealed in pink-bricked alcoves and the walls were covered with old posters advertising opera or long-gone art exhibitions.

'Don't you think,' said Armand at last, 'that if Oliver does not like Monsieur Jackson his anxiety could simply have come from *monsieur's* talk of buying a property and the possibility of living with him?'

'That possibility hadn't been discussed with Oliver,' said Gaby.

'Children can be very perceptive...'

'But it hadn't even been decided between Martin and me, for heaven's sake!'

'Maybe not.' Armand shrugged. 'But the possibility was there, and perhaps that was enough to bring on anxiety—especially in a child who has already known trauma in his life.'

'Trauma...?'

'Losing his father?' Armand raised his eyebrows. 'Enough truama, I would say, to last a very long time...'

Gaby fell silent again, watching the wax run from the candle to add to the encrusted mass around the bottle. 'You really think it might have been that?' she said at last, looking up. 'The prospect of living with Martin brought on Oliver's asthma?'

Armand shrugged again, the gesture in itself sufficient answer.

'Well, if it was that—' Gaby took a deep breath '—there's little likelihood of it happening again.'

'What do you mean?' Armand had been about to take more paté, but he stopped, his knife poised, and looked at her.

'I've told Martin I don't want our relationship to continue.' She spoke quietly and Armand continued to stare at her. The sounds of the restaurant and of the other diners continued around them, but it was as if they were alone, in a void of their own making. 'It was you, Armand, who really made me think,' she said at last.

The expression in his eyes changed, darkened. 'Me?' he said.

Gaby had no way of knowing whether his surprise was feigned or genuine. 'Yes,' she said softly, 'when you told me to be careful not to rush into something for the wrong reasons. It made me examine my feelings. I knew I'd been attracted to Martin because of his resemblance to Terry. I had also come to realise since I'd got to know him better that he was, in fact, nothing like Terry.' She paused and began absent-mindedly scoring grooves on the white tablecloth with her thumbnail.

Armand remained silent, as if allowing her time to get her thoughts into order.

'I had also recognised that I couldn't live with him,' Gaby went on at last, then, abandoning the pattern she was making on the cloth, she looked up sharply. 'Again, Armand, it was something you said that had made me think.'

'I seem to have been responsible for many things,' murmured Armand, raising one eyebrow. 'So what else did I say?'

'It was when you asked if Martin had mentioned marriage, and said that if he hadn't it was an insult to myself and to Oliver to assume that I would simply live with him—I'd not really thought of it like that before.'

'Ah,' said Armand. 'If a man has all he needs, it may never become necessary for him to change.'

Gaby frowned. 'Are you are saying that if I'd lived with Martin I may never have become his wife?'

'Something like that.' Armand laughed, his teeth white against his olive complexion.

Gaby frowned, intrigued for a moment, then slowly said, 'I think I might have been prepared to accept that...' She paused, then impulsively she added, 'But what you really made me ask myself was what I would have done if Martin *had* asked me to marry him.'

'And?' Armand leaned forward again, not taking his eyes from hers as he waited for her reply.

The silence they had created around them seemed suddenly heightened, the sounds of the restaurant even more remote.

'I would have said no,' she said.

'Do you know why?' Again the quizzical raising of his eyebrow. 'After all, he would have offered security...a home...would presumably have been a father to Oliver.'

'I would have said no,' she said quietly, 'because I don't love him.'

'Ah!' Armand sat back in his chair. '*L'amour*,' he murmured.

'I suppose I thought I might have grown to love him,' said Gaby after a while. 'But it's not enough,' she added passionately. 'At least, for me it isn't.'

'You loved your husband, Gabrielle?'

'Oh, yes,' she whispered, looking down at the tablecloth. 'I loved Terry.'

'So you know about love, would recognise it if it came along again?' Putting his elbows on the table, Armand rested his chin on his hands, willing her, she sensed, to look at him.

'Yes.' She looked up then, and found herself looking directly into his eyes. 'Oh, yes,' she added, allowing her gaze to move, to wander over the sensual curve of his mouth. 'I'm sure I would. I suppose I had conditioned myself into believing it could never happen that way again—not twice in one lifetime.'

'*Madame*? *Monsieur*?'

Abruptly they drew apart, looking up to find a bemused waiter trying to find space on their table for their main course.

They ate duck—succulent slices in a piquant redcurrant sauce with asparagus tips—followed by soft cheeses—goat's cheese and Roquefort—then fruit—fresh peaches, figs and apricots.

They talked shop for a while, about OBEX, and the advantages and disadvantages of working for an industrial medical team. Inevitably the subject turned to Gaby's work, and Gaby, possibly fortified by the red wine, found herself boldly asking Armand about his reluctance to accept counselling. When he didn't immediately reply, she said, 'As I've told you before—you're not the first doctor I have encountered with the same aversion. Maybe doctors simply see it as some sort of threat.'

'Not in my case,' Armand replied.

'Yet you were sceptical? You have to admit that,' she persisted.

'Yes,' he nodded. 'I confess I was. But I have come to realise it is the quality of the counselling that counts—and that, of course, depends on the skill of the counsellor.'

She frowned. 'That sounds as if you've had experience of a bad one.'

'Not me, personally,' Armand replied slowly, then admitted, 'But, yes, someone close to me. And as far as I am concerned bad counselling can be more harmful than no counselling at all.'

'I agree,' replied Gaby swiftly, then fell silent, thinking that he would not wish to discuss the matter further if it was personal.

'It was Monique,' he said abruptly.

'Your sister-in-law?'

He nodded. 'Yes, she was in a car crash. She lost the child she was carrying—a much wanted daughter. She couldn't come to terms with it. Counselling was suggested but. . .' He shrugged.

'It was unhelpful?' asked Gaby quietly.

'In my opinion it did more harm than good,' he replied tightly. 'Monique is still traumatised, and cannot face the prospect of another pregnancy.' He fell silent then, but to Gaby it explained so much.

Their conversation switched to Gaby's hometown of Branchester, and the house she had lived in with her mother, then, as they lingered over *café au lait*, Armand once again mentioned his own family.

'I would like you to meet them,' he said stirring his coffee.

Gaby had been about to take a sip of her own coffee, but she paused and stared at him, then set the cup down again. 'Meet them?' she said suddenly, aware that her heart was thumping.

Martin had accused her of finishing their relationship because of Armand's influence; she had denied it, had refused even to consider that Armand might be interested in her, but, if that was the case, was it not strange that he should be suggesting she meet his family?

'Yes.' He was nodding now, and Gaby found herself looking at him closely—the proud, almost arrogant tilt of his head, the handsome profile and dark colouring, the expensive clothes and undeniable air of impeccable breeding—and she wondered about this family of his. 'Yes,' he went on, oblivious of her appraisal, 'I would like to take you and Oliver to Château Laurent.'

'Château?' she asked weakly, her imagination beginning to run riot as she recalled films she'd seen of the French Revolution and the sumptuous fairy tale châteaux of the wealthy aristocracy.

'I told you—my family own a vineyard.' A smile touched his lips as he caught sight of her expression. 'It is in the Gaillac region...not too far from here. Maybe we could go—perhaps one weekend? My nephews would be delighted to meet Oliver, and I am sure he would enjoy it.'

'I don't doubt it,' murmured Gaby.

'And you, Gabrielle.' He reached out and touched her hand where it lay on the white tablecloth. She felt her whole body quiver in response to his touch. 'I think you would enjoy it too.'

Again she allowed her eyes to meet his. 'I think I would as well,' she agreed. She had tried to keep her tone casual, but feared she had failed miserably.

'I think. . .' he went on, not attempting to release her hand, 'I think we like many things the same.'

She smiled. 'Well, we certainly have the same taste in music. . .Unless—' she threw him a mischievous glance from beneath her eyelashes '—unless you were pretending to enjoy the concert to please me.'

'Do you think I was pretending?' As he spoke he increased the pressure of his hand.

'No,' she said softly, 'I think you enjoyed it as much as I did.'

'You think you would know if I was pretending?' Gently he began to caress the back of her hand with his thumb.

'I hope I would.' Her reply was light and—again, she hoped—casual, betraying nothing of the turmoil he was creating inside her.

'Just as I am sure I would know if you were pretending,' he said softly. 'But I cannot imagine, Gabrielle, there would ever be the need for pretence between us.' He released her hand then, and, looking up, caught the waiter's eye and summoned him to their table.

On leaving the restaurant they strolled through a narrow back street lit by a single old-fashioned lamp, their footsteps ringing out in the silence as they passed darkened, shuttered houses until they reached the place where Armand had left the car.

He did not take her straight home, driving instead through the city, so that Gaby could see Toulouse by night. He finally stopped the car on the embankment and pointed out the darkened outline of a bridge spanning the river. 'Le Pont Neuf,' he murmured, slipping one arm around Gaby's shoulders. The movement was so natural, so casual, and the pressure of his arm felt so right that she made no comment, instead moving her head slightly, so that as he leaned towards her she rested against him.

I am, she thought, only half listening as he named landmarks, at this moment totally happy. If only life could go on like this.

As if sensing her mood, as if completely in tune with her thoughts, Armand fell silent, and it came as no surprise to Gaby when she felt his hand beneath her chin, tilting her face towards him.

She had known that he was going to kiss her, had anticipated it from the moment she had stepped into his car and she had seen the look in his eyes. She had known it when they had sat close together in the cloisters letting the music of Chopin and Schubert wash over them, and she had known it all the time they had faced each other across the restaurant table.

Neither was she disappointed as she closed her eyes and felt his lips on hers. His kiss was gentle at first, like that other occasion when he had kissed her, but there the similarity ended, for as her lips parted in response it grew more urgent, filled with the promise of a passion that thrilled and delighted her. His hands became entangled in her hair as his kiss grew deeper, more demanding, and in the end it was with an apology, muttered in French, that he drew sharply away from her.

'I think,' he said, 'I should take you home—or I may not be responsible for what might happen.' He laughed then, but it was a shaky laugh, and Gaby knew that he was deeply moved, just as she herself was moved by what was happening between them. As far as she was concerned his apology was totally unnecessary, and if it had been left to her she would have been quite happy for him to continue, whether he would be responsible for his actions or not.

The very idea of Armand Laurent out of control set her pulse racing even faster.

She was just wondering how she could convey that to him without appearing completely wanton when, to her disappointment, he fastened his seat belt and switched on the engine.

With a sigh she leaned against the headrest as they left the embankment, having to console herself with simply gazing at his profile as he drove her home.

CHAPTER TEN

SUNDAY seemed to drag into infinity. Whereas for most it was a welcome day off, for Gaby it couldn't end fast enough—for its end would mean the coming of Monday. Monday meant work, work meant OBEX—and OBEX meant Armand.

If there had been any doubt in her mind about her interest in Armand it had been swept away on Saturday night. In fact, she told herself ruefully as she drove to work on Monday morning, there was a very real danger that she was on the point of falling in love with him.

She had not felt like this since those first heady days with Terry—the anticipation, the stomach-churning, the counting of hours followed by that wonderful moment when you caught sight of a certain man and your heart turned over.

She had certainly never felt that way with Martin, she thought sadly as she parked the car in the factory car park and switched off the engine. At the time she had thought it was because it never happened that way a second time, but meeting Armand had disproved that theory.

'Well, good morning.' At first Gaby thought the voice that broke into her thoughts belonged to one of the workmen building the new office block, but most of those men were French, and this voice, with its edge of sarcasm, was unmistakably English. When she looked up it was to find Martin peering in the car window.

'Hello, Martin,' she said. Her heart sank as he waited while she picked up her briefcase from the back seat, got out of the car and locked the door.

'Good weekend?' he asked as they began to walk across the car park.

'Yes, very, thank you.' She kept her reply brief, not wanting to be drawn into conversation with him, fearing that it might lead to an argument—which was the last thing she wanted, here in the car park in full view of the office windows.

Martin, however, seemed to have other ideas. 'Thought I might have seen you on Saturday night at Dave Thomas' place,' he said. 'You missed a great party.'

'I wasn't invited,' she murmured.

'You don't have to wait for an invitation to these things—you just turn up. You should know that by now. I quite expected to see you there,' he went on, when she didn't reply. 'I thought you'd have begun to realise that you were missing me...'

Still Gaby didn't answer. By this time they had reached the double doors of the main entrance. Once on the other side she knew that she could make her escape as they would go in different directions.

'So what did you do?' he asked as he held the door open for her.

'I'm sorry?' She feigned innocence, knowing full well what he meant.

'On Saturday night? I suppose you just stayed home.'

Something in his attitude suddenly stung her. 'No, Martin,' she said as she passed him in the doorway. 'As it happens, I didn't just stay at home. I went to a concert.'

'Concert?' He frowned, then, letting the doors swing shut behind them, he moved round in front of her so that he barred her path. 'What concert?'

'At the Jacobin cloisters,' she replied patiently.

He stared at her in apparent amazement. 'You went to a concert—on your own?' he demanded.

'No, Martin, not on my own,' she replied patiently, then, aware that his eyes had narrowed slightly, she added, 'Armand—Dr Laurent took me.'

She saw the flicker in his eyes, then for a long moment he continued to stare at her. At last, very quietly, he said, 'So I was right. Laurent *was* the reason you ditched me.'

Gaby took a deep breath. 'No, Martin,' she said, 'it wasn't like that at all.'

'So what was it like?' Gaby thought that she detected a slightly menacing note in his voice, and as she tried to edge past him he stood firm, forcing her to remain where she was. 'Come on,' he said, 'tell me—what is it with this smoothie French guy?'

Finally, realising that he wasn't going to let her pass without some sort of explanation, she said, 'Armand simply knew how much I was missing my music, that's all, Martin. Now, please, I really must go. I have work to do.' Still she thought that he wasn't going to move, then to her relief he stood to one side, and at last she managed to get past him. But as she walked away from him he couldn't resist a parting shot.

'You'll live to regret it,' he said, and there was no mistaking the ugly note in his voice now. 'You mark my words, Gaby, you'll live to regret it. They're not like us—their ways are different. But if you want to find out the hard way that's up to you—just don't say I didn't warn you!'

As she walked down the corridor she was only too aware that he continued to stand there watching her.

When she reached the medical unit her thoughts were still in turmoil. The last thing she had intended had been to hurt Martin. She still felt grateful to him for encouraging her to take the first step towards a new life for herself and Oliver, and she had hoped that even after ending their relationship they might remain friends. Now it seemed as if Martin hadn't even accepted the fact that their relationship really was at an end. The impression she had gained from their conversation was that he had been waiting for her to come to her senses, and she was also only too aware of his contempt for Armand.

She was still battling with her thoughts as she walked into Julie Roberts' office and found her in consultation with Armand.

They both looked up, and as Gaby met Armand's gaze her senses reeled, taking yet another battering.

'*Bonjour*!' he murmured.

'Hello, Gaby,' said Julie, mercifully apparently unaware of the strong undercurrent between her two colleagues. 'We were just talking about Tom Shackleton. He was all set to drive himself to the hospital this morning, but Armand doesn't think that's a good idea. I don't suppose you're free?' she added hopefully.

'I'm sorry, I'm afraid I have an early appointment,' said Gaby, lowering her gaze from Armand's, unable to cope with what she saw there. 'I have Justin Metcalf coming in—and, I hope, bringing his girlfriend Claudine with him.'

'In that case,' said Julie briskly, 'I'll take Tom, and Suzanne can assist Armand with surgery. Oh, and Gaby—' Julie picked up a folder from the desk and handed it to her '—could you see this girl, please? She's a secretary—desperately wanted to come here to work, but is now suffering from what sounds like an acute case of homesickness. Armand and I think it would help if she could talk to you.'

'Very well.' Gaby took the folder and turned to the door. 'I must get on,' she said then, as the phone rang and Julie turned to answer it. Armand joined her and they left the office together.

'Is there anything wrong?' he asked as he closed the door behind him. He spoke quietly so that Luc, who was checking supplies in the store room, could not hear.

'Wrong?' Gaby had been about to retreat to her consulting room, but she paused. 'What makes you think there's anything wrong?'

'When you came into the office you looked. . .how you say it. . .?' Armand hesitated, searching for the right word, then said, 'Flustered. . .yes, that is it. . . flustered.'

'I. . .' For a moment Gaby was at a loss to know what to say to him. How could she tell him that she had been upset because Martin might have inadvertently hit upon the truth over her reasons for ending her relationship with him?

'Had someone upset you?' Armand persisted, when still she floundered for an answer.

'In a way,' she admitted at last.

'So who was it?'

'Oh, no one. It was nothing,' she protested, 'really it wasn't.'

'Yes, it was. You were upset. Someone had upset you. I want to know, Gabrielle,' he said. 'I don't like to see you upset.'

'Well. . .' She hesitated. 'It was Martin, actually. . .'

'Ah, Monsieur Jackson.' Armand nodded. 'I thought it might be him.'

'No, you don't understand. . .really, it wasn't anything. . .' Gaby protested, further alarmed now by the angry glint that had come into Armand's eyes.

'Maybe Monsieur Jackson is not happy with the fact that you finish your relationship with him—that you go out with me. . . Is that it, Gabrielle?' he asked, then, when she remained silent, he went on, 'I see I may have hit on the truth. Do not let him upset you,' he added, lightly touching her arm.

She allowed herself to look up at him then, and as their eyes met once more suddenly Gaby wished they were anywhere other than in the busy medical unit, where patients were beginning to arrive for surgery. For a moment it seemed as if Armand, too, was wishing the same thing, for he moved closer and very slightly lowered his head.

When it seemed that he might be about to ignore what was going on around them and flout convention, Gaby gave a murmured exclamation and, not giving him a chance to say or do anything further, turned away and fled from the unit, down the corridor to the sanctuary of her room.

With her heart still thumping wildly she barely had time to sort her case-notes for the day before someone knocked on the door. She thought for a moment that it was Armand, that he had followed her, and when she called out for whoever it was to come in, and Justin Metcalf appeared, she didn't know whether she was relieved or disappointed.

'Morning.' Justin nodded without smiling.

'Hello, Justin. Come in,' said Gaby, desperately struggling to recover her composure, then, looking beyond him, she frowned. 'Isn't Claudine with you?' she asked.

Justin shook his head and, coming right into the room, shut the door behind him. 'No,' he said, sitting down in the chair opposite Gaby. 'No, she said she didn't want to come.'

'That's a pity,' said Gaby. 'Did she say why?'

'She said there weren't no need.'

'I don't quite understand.' Gaby leaned forward and glanced at Justin's notes. 'You first approached us—the medical team,' she went on after a moment, 'because Claudine is pregnant—isn't that so?'

'Yeah.' Justin nodded.

'And Claudine wanted a termination?'

He nodded again. 'Yeah,' he said, then muttered, 'Well, I thought she did.'

'And now?' asked Gaby.

'Looks like I was wrong, don't it? She says she wants to keep it—I think it's because her old man's been going on at her. . .' He shrugged.

Gaby stared thoughtfully at him for a moment, then said, 'And what about you, Justin?'

'Me?' He looked up sharply and she saw the defiance in his dark eyes. 'What d'you mean?'

'Well, it's your baby as well,' she said quietly.

'Yeah, I know. But, like I told you, it was an accident. I didn't mean it to happen, and the way I see it she's the one who wants it—not me. I told you, I'm not into marriage and all that, didn't I?'

'Yes, that's right, you did,' agreed Gaby, then, watching him closely, she said, 'Did you tell Claudine that as well?'

'Yeah, she knew.' He nodded again. 'So it's like I say—if she wants to keep the kid, it's up to her. I was prepared to help her—I came here, didn't I?'

He paused for a long moment and they sat in silence, then almost angrily he said, 'But if she don't want no help there's not a lot I can do about it, is there?'

'What about her parents, Justin?'

'Her parents?' He had begun to gnaw the side of his thumbnail, but he stopped and threw Gaby a sharp glance. 'What about her parents?'

'How are they reacting now?'

'Well, I told you—her old man went demented when he found out.'

'Yes, I can imagine.'

'You'd think in this day and age people would be used to this sort of thing...wouldn't you?'

'They probably had other plans for their daughter, Justin.'

'Yeah, well, they should think about what *she* wants, and not what they want...that's the trouble with families. My old man was just the same...always going on about getting qualifications, as if that were the be all and end all—'

'So what is it that Claudine wants?' asked Gaby, quietly interrupting.

'Eh?' Justin shot her a look from beneath his dark eyebrows.

'You said Claudine's parents should let her do what she wants. Do you know what that is?'

He looked bewildered, and Gaby went on, 'Let's put it another way. If, as you say, Claudine wants to keep the baby, what are *you* going to do, Justin?'

'Oh!' He looked relieved. 'I'm going back to England.'

'Really?' Gaby raised her eyebrows.

'Yeah.' He nodded. 'Me contract ends soon.'

'So you don't have any plans to apply for a new contract in Toulouse?'

'Nah, shouldn't think so—get back to me mates...' He shrugged. ''Spect I will, anyway. Not much choice really, is there?'

'There's always a choice, Justin,' she said quietly.

He stared at her, but remained silent.

'What will you do in the meantime?'

'What d'you mean?' He looked suspicious.

'Will you still be seeing Claudine?'

''Course I will.' He said it indignantly, as if affronted that she should think otherwise.

'Well, Justin—' Gaby took a deep breath '—it looks as if you've sorted things out, so I don't really think there's anything I can do for you.'

'No. Right, well, thanks anyway, Mrs Dexter.'

'That's all right, Justin—' She broke off as an alarm bell suddenly sounded through the building, startling them both.

'Emergency!' Justin leapt to his feet and wrenched open the door, then he dived outside into the corridor.

Gaby followed, running to keep up as Justin disappeared through the swing doors at the end of the corridor. When she burst through the doors she found him looking through a glass partition down onto the factory floor.

'What is it?' she demanded. 'Justin?'

'I don't know,' he muttered. 'I can't see anything.' He started to run again. 'You'd better stay here,' he yelled over his shoulder.

'No, I'll come with you. I'm a nurse.' Gaby, too, began to run, down the corridor towards the metal staircase to the factory floor. At the top of the stairs Justin suddenly stopped. 'It could be a fire,' he said.

'All the more reason why they may need me,' she said, fighting her own fear but at the same time touched by his concern for her.

The alarm was still ringing as Gaby began to descend the stairs. She saw Justin jump the last half-dozen stairs to the factory floor, and at the same time she became aware of the sound of running footsteps, of warning shouts. Then she realised that people were running not onto the factory floor, as she had imagined, but out of the building.

She joined them—running outside, blinking in the strong sunlight. Then, crossing the grounds, she saw people converging on an area beside the new office block. As she ran Gaby suddenly realised that Armand was beside her.

'What is it?' she gasped. 'What's happened?'

'An accident,' he shouted. 'A lorry, I think.'

They rounded the corner of the new block and were able to see for themselves what had happened. A lorry carrying a mass of timber rafters had shed its load. The mountain of wood was lying on the ground in front of the partly constructed building.

As they approached Armand stifled an exclamation, then, to Gaby's horror, between the rafters she caught glimpses of coloured material.

The next few minutes were a blur as the workforce who had run from the factory floor began to lift the topmost rafters one by one to get closer to the men trapped underneath.

Gaby, watching helplessly, knowing that she was not strong enough to lift the wood, saw Armand grab Justin's arm, pulling him back as the younger man would have dived straight into the mass to lift the rafters pinning the men to the ground.

As they were joined by more and more of the OBEX workforce Armand took command, carefully climbing across the remaining rafters and speaking to the trapped men, trying to assess their injuries. Moments later he gave instructions to the rescuers on how to lift the wood without causing further damage, and as the pile was rapidly shifted two injured men were eventually released.

Gaby, who was watching Armand, saw him beckon to Justin, who scrambled to join him, then together they gently lifted the final rafter that had been pinning a third man to the ground. Armand bent over the man for a moment, then, straightening up, he turned and looked in Gaby's direction.

Instinctively she knew what he wanted and, picking up his medical case from the ground, she climbed across the wood to join him.

'I need to give morphine to this man,' he said.

Gaby opened his case and took out antiseptic pads, disposable syringes and ampoules of morphine. She drew up an injection, and as she passed it to Armand Luc and Suzanne arrived in the factory ambulance.

Armand instructed Luc in rapid French to attend to the other two injured men then turned back to the third man and administered the painkilling injection. Gaby, kneeling on the ground beside Armand, saw that the man was probably in his late fifties, whereas the other two were much younger.

'His thorax is crushed,' muttered Armand as the man began moaning softly.

'Dr Laurent!' Luc was suddenly beside them again. 'The man over there—' he pointed to one of the two men on the ground '—he has severe lacerations to his left leg and he's bleeding badly.'

Armand looked up. 'Stay here, Gabrielle,' he said. 'Luc, get oxygen to this man, please.'

While Armand scrambled back across the rafters Gaby talked softly to the older man, trying to reassure him as he fought for breath. Whether he understood English or not she didn't know, but he seemed comforted simply by the sound of her voice.

Luc was back almost immediately with the oxygen cylinder from the factory ambulance. He handed Gaby the mask, and while he operated the gauge on the cylinder she placed the mask over the man's face to assist his breathing.

It could only have been moments later that Armand returned, but to Gaby it seemed like hours, for she had lived each laboured breath the injured Frenchman had taken.

'How is he?' Armand, his stethoscope round his neck, leaned across the man.

'Not good,' murmured Gaby. 'I thought at first the oxygen was helping him—but now. . .' She shook her head.

Armand pressed the stethoscope to the man's chest and listened. 'Pneumothorax,' he muttered after a moment. 'His lung has collapsed.'

'You want to move him?' Luc threw a quick glance towards the waiting factory ambulance, but Armand shook his head. 'I need to remove the pressure,' he said as the man's breathing became even more laboured.

Luc nodded, and once more ran to the ambulance.

'The other man?' Gaby glanced across to where Suzanne was kneeling beside one of the injured men.

'He will be all right,' said Armand. 'Suzanne is applying pressure to the artery to stop the bleeding.'

'What do you want me to do?' Gaby glanced at the last of the injured men, who was sitting propped against the wall nursing his arm. Justin was beside him while yet another employee was trying to calm the distraught lorry driver.

'Stay here,' said Armand. 'I need to do a thoracotomy—I may need your help.'

Gaby nodded, then took the man's hand and began talking to him again.

Luc returned with the equipment Armand needed from the ambulance and still Gaby talked, asking the man about his family, telling him about hers, about Oliver, about her mother, about England, about anything that came into her head—anything to try to distract him. By now he was drowsy from the morphine, but the incision Armand made in his side would still come as a shock, in spite of a shot of local anaesthetic.

She carried on talking, the man's eyes never leaving her face as Armand inserted the probe deep into his lung, attached the tubing and began to draw off fluid. She talked all the while she assisted Armand to set up an intravenous infusion, and even after the outside ambulances arrived she held the man's hand, and still she talked, quietly reassuring him.

A little later, closely supervised by Armand, the man was lifted onto a stretcher and carried into one of the waiting vehicles, then, along with the other two injured men and the lorry driver—who by this time was suffering from severe shock—he was driven away.

The sound of the ambulance sirens faded into the distance and the men who had helped to shift the wood began to restack it. Someone started up the lorry and moved it, Luc and Suzanne walked back to their ambulance, and Armand turned to Gaby, who, still kneeling on the ground, had just gathered up the contents of his case.

'Enough excitement, I think, for one day,' he said, looking down at her.

She nodded, stood up and handed him the case. 'You're right,' she said.

'Thank you for your help,' he said quietly as they began to walk back to the factory.

She shrugged. 'I didn't do much.'

'I tend to forget you are a qualified nurse.' Armand ran a hand through his short dark hair.

'So do I.' She gave a wry smile. 'I don't get to do much hands-on nursing these days.'

'You calmed that man so much you almost hypnotised him,' said Armand. 'As far as I am concerned reassurance is as important a part of nursing as anything else. You seem to have a calming effect on people—I am beginning to understand, Gabrielle, why you were so highly recommended as a counsellor.'

His words brought a warm glow to her heart, especially coming as they did from a man who had doubted the benefits of counselling. Gaby was still basking in the warmth of his unexpected praise when they reached the factory doors and Justin caught them up.

Armand turned. 'You did well,' he said.

'I didn't do a lot,' Justin muttered.

'You probably helped save a man's life,' said Armand.

'Yeah, well...' Justin gave an embarrassed shrug, then said with a frown, 'It shouldn't have happened, though, should it, Doc?'

Armand shook his head. 'I shall be calling for an inquiry. Have you any theories as to how or why it might have happened?' He glanced at Justin. 'You must have been one of the first on the scene.'

'I guess the rope holding the wood broke.' Justin frowned. 'But if that's the case it weren't strong enough in the first place, were it?'

'Exactly,' replied Armand. As they entered the factory he and Gaby turned towards the medical unit and Justin towards the shop floor, then suddenly Justin stopped.

'Had you finished with me, Mrs Dexter?' he asked.

'Yes, I think so, Justin,' Gaby replied. 'Unless, of course—' she paused, '—you would like to come back for another chat. Maybe when you've decided whether or not you are going to return to England.'

Justin nodded, then glanced at Armand. 'Mrs Dexter's brilliant,' he said. 'She doesn't exactly tell you what to do...but...'

'She gives you some idea of what you *could* do? Is that it?' asked Armand.

Justin frowned. 'I don't think she even does that—she says everyone should be free to make their own choice.' Shaking his head, he disappeared down the passage to the factory.

'Another sign of a good counsellor?' murmured Armand as he and Gaby began to walk towards the medical unit. 'Let the patient think the decision he makes is entirely his own idea?'

Gaby raised her eyebrows and smiled.

'Were you counselling Justin when the accident happened?' Armand went on after a moment.

Gaby nodded. 'Yes, then the alarm sounded and all hell broke loose.'

'Did Claudine Flaubert come with him?' Armand asked suddenly, as if he had just remembered.

'No. . .' Gaby paused. 'You were quite right, though, about Claudine not wanting a termination.'

Armand threw her a quick glance but remained silent.

'Apparently she's changed her mind,' Gaby went on. 'That is if she ever did want one in the first place. Or else it was simply Justin assuming that was what she wanted.'

'That was probably more like it,' Armand commented. 'So what is happening now?' he said after a moment.

'Justin says it's up to Claudine what she does,' replied Gaby. 'But he says he's going back to England.'

'And do you think he'll go?'

'Time will tell. . .' Gaby trailed off, leaving the sentence unfinished as they entered the medical unit.

Julie had just returned from the hospital with Tom Shackleton, and Suzanne was telling them about the accident.

'For God's sake!' Tom looked appalled. 'I turn my back for five minutes. . .! How many men were injured?' He turned to Armand.

Out of the corner of her eye Gaby saw Mélisande come into the room.

'Three,' replied Armand. 'One man has a crushed

chest and a collapsed lung, another severe lacerations to his thigh, and the third had a fractured arm—they are all on their way to hospital.'

'What the hell happened?' Tom still looked stricken.

'We do not know.' Armand shrugged.

'Was there a breach of safety regulations?'

'I do not think so,' replied Armand. 'It would seem that the timber fell from the lorry because it was not properly secured, or because the rope holding it was not strong enough. Either would be the responsibilty of the contractor and nothing to do with OBEX. . . But of course there will be an inquiry.'

Tom sank down onto a chair and passed one hand over his face. Gaby felt sorry for him, then suddenly Suzanne said, 'How did you get on at the hospital, Tom?'

He looked up in bewilderment, as if for the moment he'd forgotten where he had been and why. While everyone waited for his answer Gaby found herself watching Mélisande, to see what her reaction would be.

'It wasn't too bad,' Tom muttered absent-mindedly at last. It seemed to Gaby as if his own troubles had been overshadowed by the morning's events.

And Mélisande's expression, although polite, remained impassive—no more and no less concerned than anyone else's. Hardly, Gaby thought, the reaction one would expect from a man's mistress.

The episode, insignificant as it might have been, only served to reinforce Gaby's opinion that Mélisande Legrande was not having an affair with Tom Shackleton.

Gaby was pleased—pleased for Penny, who loved Tom so much, and pleased because she, too, had once known what it was to love someone. Cautiously she allowed her gaze to wander to Armand. Could it be that she was about to love again?

As if he sensed her gaze on him, Armand turned his head. Their eyes met and Gaby felt a thrill—a thrill that was becoming so familiar when he was around that she could almost have been forgiven for thinking that it was becoming a habit.

CHAPTER ELEVEN

'Look, Mum, there she is—under that branch!' Oliver pointed excitedly, and when Gaby bent down she could see on the opposite side of the stream the tawny neck and head of a duck. 'And she's got babies,' he went on. 'We saw them this afternoon.'

'In that case I think we should leave her in peace,' said Gaby, taking Oliver's hand and gently drawing him away. 'If she gets frightened she might leave her babies, and we don't want that to happen.'

'We could look after them,' said Oliver, with one last reluctant look over his shoulder as they began walking away from the stream and into the poppyfield.

'I don't think we would do so well as their mother,' said Gaby, 'and I dare say their dad is around somewhere as well.'

'I wish I had a dad,' said Oliver suddenly.

Gaby shot him a quick glance. His hair was tousled, his lower lip thrust out, and he looked so like Terry that her heart ached. Only this time, she realised with surprise, the ache was more for Oliver than for Terry. She searched for something she could say about Terry, imagining that that was what Oliver wanted to hear, but before she could think of anything he said, 'When can I go and play with Dr Laurent's soldiers again?'

'Oh. . .' She was taken aback for a moment. 'I don't know, Oliver.'

'When are you going for another lesson?' he asked eagerly.

'Tomorrow, but. . .'

'Oh, brill!'

'But I don't know if you can come every time. Dr Laurent said you could come if there was no one here to look after you. . .'

'He won't mind,' said Oliver. 'I know he won't. And he said to me I could go whenever I liked.'

'Well. . .I don't know. . .' said Gaby doubtfully.

'But will you ask him?' Oliver persisted.

'I don't think I shall see him before then. He doesn't have a surgery tomorrow. I hardly saw him today,' she added, more to herself than to Oliver. 'It was a very busy day at the factory, and Dr Laurent was in surgery all the time. . .' She trailed off and turned as she realised that Oliver had stopped. He was staring up the field, shading his eyes from the sun.

'There's someone coming,' he said.

Gaby, too, raised both hands and shaded her eyes, but all she could see was the dark outline of a figure at the very top of the field as it made its way towards them. In the end she wasn't sure what came first—her realisation or Oliver's shout.

'It's Dr Laurent! Oh, brill, now we can ask him!'

Her heart thumping, she watched him walk towards them. He was wearing denims and a red shirt casually open at the neck and turned back at the cuffs.

'I was told I would find you here.' He smiled at Oliver, then his gaze sought hers.

'This is a surprise,' she said lightly, at the same time trying desperately not to let him see just how welcome a surprise it was.

'I came to talk to Tom and Penny,' he said simply. 'Then I thought I should find the pair of you to remind Oliver he can come with you tomorrow if he wishes.'

'I told you!' Oliver whispered, tugging at the sleeve of her loose cotton blouse. 'I said it would be all right.'

'Yes,' she agreed weakly, 'you did.'

'That what would be all right?' Armand, looking mystified, glanced from one to the other.

'For Oliver to come with me tomorrow,' said Gaby.

'I told you,' Armand replied. 'He can come whenever he likes.'

'See!' Oliver said excitedly, then he began to run on ahead. 'I'm going to tell Harry,' he shouted over his shoulder.

'You've made his day,' murmured Gaby.

'I thought I made it plain he could come to my house

whenever he wishes.' Armand looked down at her, the light catching the green flecks in his dark eyes.

'I don't want him to think he can take advantage. . .'

'He won't be,' he said firmly.

She smiled, hesitated, then said, 'You said you came to talk to Tom and Penny—is everything all right?'

'I came to talk about the excision,' he said quietly. 'The melanoma was malignant.'

'I feared it might be,' she admitted, then, turning abruptly away from him, she stared at the beauty of the surrounding countryside, thinking how cruel nature could sometimes be.

'He will need further treatment,' said Armand after a while. 'But there is every hope that all the cells will be eradicated.'

'How are they taking it?' Gaby glanced towards the house.

'Very well, really—they will face it together, whatever happens. . .' He paused, indicating another path that meandered back to the stream, and said, 'Shall we walk awhile?'

Gaby nodded. She didn't want to go back to the house—especially at that precise moment. They began to stroll along the pathway, the fullness of her cream skirt brushing the overhanging heads of the poppies.

'Did you know they've been going through a rough patch in their marriage?' she asked after a few moments.

'What is this. . .rough patch?' Armand looked puzzled.

'A bad time,' Gaby explained. 'Not getting on. . .'

'Ah, yes.' He nodded to show that he understood what she meant, then, growing serious, he said, 'I did not know—not for sure—but I guessed as much.' He paused, then added, 'Surely all marriages have these times?'

'That's true,' she agreed, then, knowing that anything she told him would be in the strictest confidence, she said, 'Penny thought Tom was having an affair.'

'Ah,' he said again, but knowingly this time. Then he

shrugged. 'Again, these things happen—but a strong marriage can survive.'

'Do *you* think Tom was having an affair?' Gaby threw him a quick glance. 'Or still is for that matter?'

'I have no idea.' Armand gave another shrug then, bending over, plucked a blade of grass and began chewing the stem. 'But if he is,' he went on after a moment, 'only they can work it out. . . But I didn't come to find you, Gabrielle, to talk about Tom and Penny. . .'

'You said you came to remind Oliver about coming with me tomorrow.' Gaby looked sideways at him from beneath her lashes.

'That is true,' he agreed. 'But it was only half the truth. I came because I wanted to see you.'

'You saw me today,' she protested lightly.

'I hardly saw you at all today,' he said, his rueful manner exactly echoing her own sentiments. 'And when I did see you either you were busy or I had yet another patient waiting to see me. . .or Julie was tackling me about hearing tests, or safety procedures, or medical tests. . .'

She laughed softly and he slipped one arm around her shoulders. 'I know,' she said, agreeing with him at last. 'It's hopeless, isn't it?'

'I knew I would be seeing you tomorrow,' he went on, 'but that wouldn't be until the evening, when you came to the house.' They had reached the band of poplars that fringed the edge of the field, and, drawing her beneath the branches, he stopped and turned her to face him. 'I couldn't wait that long,' he said simply. 'I had to see you today. It became the most important thing in the world that I see you today—do you understand that?'

'Oh, yes, Armand,' she sighed. 'I understand.'

He gave her no chance to say anything more, instead drawing her into his arms and covering her mouth with his.

Her response was instantaneous, as natural as if they had known each other for ever instead of for only a few short weeks. Parting her lips, she welcomed him, thrilling to the sweet penetration of his kiss and the growing urgency of his embrace.

Above them, the sunlight, still warm in spite of the lateness of the hour, filtered through the leaves, catching the brightness of Gaby's hair.

And then, as Armand's kiss grew deeper, Gaby felt the stirring of desire deep inside her—a desire she had not felt for a very long time, a desire she thought had died along with Terry, in the flames aboard the oil rig. She had always imagined in the intervening years that any future relationship she had would be different, with none of the passion she had shared with Terry. Her relationship with Martin had seemed to bear out that theory. But now here it was again, in the arms of this Frenchman—a desire clamouring for fulfilment.

When at last Armand lifted his head he looked down at her while continuing to hold her close in the protecting circle of his arms.

'This colour you are wearing—' gently he touched the aquamarine of her blouse '—it suits you so well... your hair... You are quite, quite beautiful, *ma chérie*.'

Gaby felt the colour touch her cheeks. No one had called her beautiful for a very long time, and on Armand's lips the words were especially precious.

Gently he cupped her face between his hands and kissed her again. She closed her eyes, allowing her arms to encircle him, her fingers to sink into his hair, only too aware, from his growing sense of urgency and the hardening of his body, of the effect she was having on him, and at the same time wishing the moment could last for ever.

In the end, to Gaby's disappointment, with a smothered groan Armand drew away from her. 'I think I must go.' He gave a shaky laugh.

'Do you have to?' she asked wistfully.

He drew a deep breath, as if struggling to regain his self-control, then said, 'Yes, I really should be going.'

'Come into the house for a while,' she said hopefully.

'I would like to, but I still have calls to make. Besides, I don't really think your hosts would want visitors tonight.'

'Probably not.' Gaby sighed. 'It's time I was getting

Oliver to bed anyway. He conveniently forgets the time if I'm not there to remind him.'

'He is a delightful child,' said Armand as they left the shelter of the trees and began slowly to make their way back through the poppies to the house.

'It's very good of you, allowing him to come to your house.'

'I told you, it really isn't a problem. Besides, I like having him around.' They walked in silence for a while, then Armand took her hand. 'I haven't forgotten,' he said, 'about you and Oliver coming to Château Laurent to meet my family. I will be speaking to my mother in a day or so—I'll see what I can arrange. That is, if you still want to come?' He stopped and turned to look at her.

'I'm surprised you need to ask,' she said softly.

By this time they had reached the front of the house, where Armand had parked his car. He turned and opened the door, then stopped.

'I almost forgot,' he said. Leaning into the car, he opened the glove compartment and took out a small package. 'This is for you.'

Gaby took the package, threw him a quick glance, then opened it. Inside was a flat box. She stared at it.

'Open it,' he said quietly.

Her fingers were trembling as she lifted the lid. On a bed of cotton wool lay the silver bangle she had admired from Lisa Rayner's collection.

For a moment she was unable to utter a word, overwhelmed that Armand had not only noticed how she had admired the bangle, but that he had taken the trouble to go and buy it for her.

'You like it?' There was slight anxiety in his tone and she looked up quickly, not wanting him to misinterpret her silence and at the same time knowing that the sudden rush of tears to her eyes would speak for themselves.

He smiled. 'You like it,' he said, satisfied by what he saw.

'It's beautiful, Armand,' she managed to whisper at last. 'Thank you. Thank you so much.'

He lifted his hand and gently ran the backs of his fingers down her cheek, then without another word he climbed into his car, fastened his seat belt, started the engine and wound down the window. 'I see you tomorrow,' he said huskily.

She watched him drive away, the dust from the path rising in a cloud behind the gleaming paintwork of his car. When he reached the end of the path he raised one hand before turning the car onto the road to Toulouse.

She hadn't wanted him to leave. She wanted to spend more time with him. Wanted to talk to him, to talk for hours, to find out everything there was to know about him. She wanted him to hold her again, wanted to feel those arms around her, to feel his lips on hers. She wanted him close to her, wanted him to love her...because... She could deny it no longer, not even to herself. She was in love with him...helplessly in love with Armand Laurent.

And, from the way he'd felt compelled to come to see her, the way he couldn't wait to be with her, from the look in his eyes when they met, the way he held her, kissed her, had to tear himself away, Gaby felt that there was a very good chance that Armand felt the same way.

At last, when the cloud of dust had settled and the sound of his car engine was little more than a hum in the distance, she turned, and with a sigh of pure happiness went into the house.

The spell of fine weather appeared to be coming to an end the following day, with great banks of dark cloud massing ominously to the west of Toulouse. By the time Gaby and Oliver drove through the archway the first low rumblings of thunder could be heard in the distance. The courtyard, as still and quiet as ever, without the sunlight seemed dark and faintly oppressive.

A small green car was parked in front of the tower beside Armand's car. It looked vaguely familiar, but for the moment Gaby couldn't think where she had seen it before. But it was not important. What was important was the fact that Armand's car was there.

The day had dragged, for the medical unit had seemed empty without him, and again Gaby had found herself counting the hours until the evening. It had been a quiet day where patients were concerned—and maybe, Gaby thought, that had been just as well. Because what with the stifling heat and the memory of what had taken place the previous evening her powers of concentration had not been quite what they should have been.

'Oh, great, Dr Laurent's here!' said Oliver as Gaby switched off the engine and he unfastened his seat belt.

'He may be busy,' said Gaby as they walked to the door and rang the bell. 'You mustn't worry him.' Then, as the door swung open and Hélène appeared, she added brightly, '*Bonjour*, Hélène.'

'*Bonjour, madame*,' replied Hélène stiffly, then, her face softening slightly, she said, '*Bonjour*, Oliver.'

'*Bonjour!*' Oliver said, and ran into the hallway. The interior was darker than ever in the strange half-light, and as Gaby followed Oliver she caught the scent of some heady perfume. It was the same scent she'd smelt on the first occasion she had come here—a scent which, she realised, with a slight sense of shock, was now familiar because she had smelt it since.

Before she had time even to think where that might have been, Hélène turned to Oliver and said, 'You may go to play with the soldiers, Oliver. Dr Laurent has someone with him at the present time.'

'I know,' said Oliver. 'It's Mélisande—I saw her car outside.'

Gaby stared at him as he ran ahead of them up the stairs.

Mélisande? Here?

Quite suddenly, like finding the last piece of a jigsaw, something fell into place. That perfume, the fragrance that still hung in the air, was not only the one she had smelt on that first occasion she had come here, it was also the one Mélisande Legrande always wore.

Slowly she began to follow Hélène up the stairs. But

there must be many women who wore that scent, she reasoned. Maybe it had been worn by a patient who had recently visited Armand... But Oliver had said the car outside belonged to Mélisande, and the car certainly had been familiar. Could that be because she saw it in the car park at the factory each day?

'Oliver,' she said, her curiosity getting the better of her as they reached the top of the stairs, 'how did you know that was Mélisande's car outside?'

He had started to run along the gallery, but he stopped and looked at her. 'Harry told me,' he said. 'We were in his mum's car one day after school and Mélisande's car was in front. Can I go now, Mum, and play with the soldiers?' He began to edge away along the gallery.

Gaby nodded, and she stared after him as he ran off. Had Penny been following Mélisande, afraid that she was meeting Tom? Was there a chance that they had been wrong, and that the French girl was having an affair with Tom after all? And what was she doing here with Armand? Could it simply be that she was his patient and was consulting him?

She was still puzzling over the situation when they reached the top of the stairs. By this time Oliver had disappeared down the corridor to the room where Armand had his battle displays. The other doors on the landing remained tightly closed.

Where was Armand?

Where was Mélisande?

Gaby was just trying to persuade herself that it was really none of her business when Hélène opened the door to her salon and stood back for her to enter the room.

'You are wondering,' she said as Gaby passed her, 'why Mélisande is here?'

Gaby paused and looked at her.

'Maybe,' Hélène went on, 'no one has taken the trouble to tell you that Mélisande Legrande is my niece.'

Gaby stared at the older woman. 'Your niece?' she said in surprise.

'I see no one has told you,' observed Hélène.

Gaby shook her head. 'I had no idea,' she said. She paused, considering, but before she could ask any questions, Hélène spoke again.

'Shall we get on with the lesson?' she asked coolly.

'Oh, yes. Yes, of course,' said Gaby. With a frown she opened her briefcase and took out her textbooks.

She would have liked to ask Hélène about Mélisande, because ever since she had come to France and to OBEX the French girl had been something of a mystery. Penny had thought she had been having an affair with Tom, then Julie had said that she was heavily involved elsewhere, but had declined to say who with. It was, however, Gaby thought as she sat down, highly unlikely that Hélène would be very forthcoming in answering questions about her niece.

This assumption was borne out by the severity of Hélène's expression as she too sat down, put on her glasses and opened her book.

Gaby's lessons with Hélène had never been easy, but that evening's proved to be more trying than most. The oppressive atmosphere didn't help, and as the rumblings of thunder grew louder with the approaching storm Gaby felt as if she'd forgotten all she had learnt. Hélène grew more and more impatient, throwing up her hands in horror at Gaby's apparent inability to master the simplest of exercises.

In the end Gaby was more than relieved when the lesson was over. All she wanted to do was to pack up her books, get out of the room and go and find Oliver and Armand. No doubt by now they would be engrossed in some military battle—the miniature soldiers drawn up into lines, the tiny flags unfurled.

But she knew that however involved Armand was, when she entered the room he would stop, he would look up, and his eyes would meet hers. . .

Her heart turned over in anticipation of the moment.

'Mélisande spends a lot of time here.' Hélène suddenly intruded into her thoughts.

Gaby glanced up and found the other woman standing watching her, her long fingers at her throat, playing with the cameo brooch that fastened her blouse.

'You say she is your niece?' asked Gaby politely. She didn't really want to talk now, didn't want to stay there, couldn't wait to go and find Armand. But she knew that it would appear rude if she was to ignore what the Frenchwoman was saying.

Hélène nodded. 'Her mother was my sister,' she said, then, her mouth twisting strangely, she added, 'She died two years ago...'

'I'm sorry...'

'I have become like a mother to Mélisande,' Hélène continued.

'She must like coming here to see you,' replied Gaby. 'And it is a beautiful house.'

'It is a beautiful house,' the Frenchwoman agreed.

Gaby couldn't help thinking that it was probably the only time Hélène had actually agreed with anything she had said.

'And, yes, Mélisande does like coming here,' Hélène went on, then she paused. 'But that,' she added, 'is because she knows that one day this house will be her home.'

Gaby had turned to the door, but at Hélène's words she stopped, one hand on the handle, thinking for a moment that she had misheard. She turned and looked at the Frenchwoman. 'I'm sorry?' she said.

'This house,' repeated Hélène with exaggerated patience. 'One day it will be Mélisande's home.'

'I don't understand.' Gaby frowned, wondering what on earth the woman meant. Was Armand thinking of selling the house? If so, would Mélisande be in a position to buy it?

'It will be Mélisande's home—' Hélène spoke clearly, deliberately '—just as soon as she marries Dr Laurent.'

Gaby stared at her. 'Marries Dr Laurent?' she said blankly.

Hélène lowered her gaze, as if suddenly she found it impossible to look Gaby in the eye. Picking up a gold pen from the table, she began toying with it.

'Mélisande and Dr Laurent are to be married,' she said at last.

A loud clap of thunder sounded directly overhead, but Gaby hardly heard it as the meaning of what Hélène was saying slowly sank in.

Mélisande and Armand to marry?

There was some mistake. There had to be. Her senses reeled, as if the world had tilted on its axis.

Mélisande was involved with someone. . . Penny had thought it was Tom. Gaby herself had disproved that, then Julie Roberts had confirmed that there was someone. . .but she hadn't said who. . .

Surely she couldn't have meant Armand?

'They grew up together.'

Gaby had to force herself to concentrate on what Hélène was saying.

'My sister, Yvonne,' she went on, when she was sure she had Gaby's attention, 'and Armand's mother, Jeanne, were great friends. Yvonne worked at Château Laurent—she kept the books—and she used to take Mélisande with her.'

Hélène's voice softened slightly, almost lost its harsh edge as her mind apparently slipped into the past. 'My niece spent her childhood with Armand and his brother Gérard. It has always been an understood fact that one day she and Armand will marry.' She looked at Gaby then, a sidelong glance. 'Did you not know this?'

Gaby, feeling as if someone had kicked her in the stomach, shook her head.

'I wondered if you were aware of the situation,' murmured Hélène. 'Armand. . .' She hesitated. 'He is like most Frenchmen—very romantic. . .very amorous; he will. . .take what is on offer. Oh, he will be generous, because that is his way, but make no mistake, the situation will not change. Things are very different here from what you may be used to. . .' She trailed off, her hands making a little fluttering gesture of dismissal.

That the Frenchwoman had just issued a warning Gaby had little doubt, but it was the implication behind the warning that brought the flush to her cheeks. The implication that Armand would use her, would take what she had to offer but would not change his marriage plans.

'I am surprised you did not know,' murmured Hélène, 'about Mélisande and Armand. It has been an accepted fact for a very long time, and with you all working at OBEX I would have thought. . .' She shrugged, leaving the sentence unfinished.

Suddenly Gaby knew that she had to get out, that she would not be responsible for what might happen if she was to stay. She had to go, to leave not only Hélène's room, which had become claustrophobic, but the house as well.

Only moments before the most important thing in the world had been that she was about to see Armand. A few murmured comments had changed that, and now all she wanted was to escape without having to face him.

'I must go,' she muttered.

Hélène inclined her head and Gaby tugged open the door and fled from the room, along the passage to the games room. As she reached the door it was suddenly flung open and Oliver stood there.

'Oh,' he said, obviously disappointed. 'I thought you were Dr Laurent. I haven't seen him yet.'

'He must be busy,' said Gaby wildly, then, taking Oliver by the hand, she pulled him out of the room and began hustling him towards the stairs.

'Mum!' he protested. 'I don't want to go yet. I haven't finished the battle.'

'I'm sorry, Oliver, but we have to get home.' She was almost running as they clattered down the stairs, Oliver struggling to keep up.

'But why?' he demanded, obviously bewildered. 'I thought we were going to see Dr Laurent. . .'

'No, Oliver,' Gaby said, more sharply than she had intended. 'Don't argue. We are going home.'

He was silent after that, but his expression was sullen. As they went out into the courtyard it started to rain, great heavy drops that spattered onto the cobblestones. The small green car was in the same place, and as they got into their own car and Gaby switched on the engine she glanced up at the house. With a sick feeling in the pit of her stomach she wondered which of the shuttered rooms Armand and Mélisande were in.

What a fool she had been. With hot tears stinging her eyes she drove smartly away, the tyres on her car squealing in protest. What a naïve little fool.

Even Oliver was silent, while, to Gaby, the courtyard which had once been so tranquil, so beautiful, now suddenly seemed sinister.

Oliver began wheezing again that night. The attack was not so bad as the previous one had been, but Gaby was forced to give him salbutamol to relieve the symptoms and to increase his dose of beclomethasone to prevent a further attack.

When at last the coughing subsided and he slept Gaby went to sit beneath the loggia. The storm had passed; it had stopped raining and there was a freshness in the air that she hadn't felt since her arrival in France. Somehow, in the aftermath of the storm, in the cool peace of evening, she needed to try to bring some order to her tangled emotions.

That she had fallen in love with Armand Laurent she had no doubt, and until this evening she could have sworn that he was beginning to feel the same way about her. If what Hélène had said was true—and in spite of the fact that she was not particularly keen on the Frenchwoman, Gaby had no reason to doubt her word—it appeared that Armand certainly shouldn't be leading her to believe that he might be falling in love with her. Because not only was his marriage to Mélisande Legrande a long-standing arrangement, it was also an imminent one.

So if he wasn't falling in love with her, what had his intentions been? Hélène had implied that he would use her—would take what was on offer, she had said, would be generous. Gaby shuddered and looked down at the silver bangle on her wrist. Had he intended keeping his relationship with Mélisande intact and conducting another, second relationship with her?

It would seem so.

Hélène had even suggested that that would have been perfectly normal—to Armand, at least. That was the way things happened here, she had said. But Gaby had detected from the older woman's manner that she had known that arrangement would be far from acceptable to her.

And surely, she agonised, Armand would have known that. He had even considered it unacceptable for Martin to ask her to live with him if he had no intention of marrying her, and in that situation there had been no other woman involved.

But there was no getting away from how it had been between her and Armand. Surely if his motives had been anything but honourable he wouldn't have shown such courtesy...been so kind to Oliver?

Unless...unless she had badly misread the situation, and his kindness had been no more than concern from one colleague for another.

Oh, God, she thought desperately, was that all it had been? Had she simply assumed more than was actually happening? She squirmed uncomfortably on her seat as she tried to recall their conversations, afraid now that she had indeed hopelessly misinterpreted the facts.

But...but when he had held her, kissed her...she could have sworn that he'd meant it. Maybe he *had* meant it. But if that was so, what of Mélisande? Did he mean it when he kissed her too?

Had Martin been right when he'd called Armand a smoothie? Was he used to having his cake and eating it? And what of the others at OBEX? Did they all know about Armand and Mélisande? Hélène had implied as much. Had they been watching what was developing between herself and the doctor? And, if so, were they laughing at her naïvety?

She shivered, pulling her cotton shawl more tightly around her shoulders, not knowing whether the cold was from a sudden chill in the air or from the bleakness of what was happening. She knew nothing of these people, she told herself bitterly. She had walked into their world with no knowledge of what had gone on before.

'Gaby?' A voice broke into her thoughts, and she looked up sharply to find that the dusk had deepened and Tom was looking down at her, an anxious expression on his face. 'What are you doing out here on your own?' he asked.

'Just thinking...'

'Oh. We wondered where you were.' He looked a little taken aback. 'There's a phone call for you.'

'Oh?' She knew who it was even before Tom spoke. 'Yes—Armand Laurent.'

She drew a deep breath. 'Would you tell him I'm not available, please, Tom?'

He continued to stare at her, and in the light that spilled out of the house through the open kitchen door Gaby could see a half-smile on his face, as if he was uncertain whether or not she was joking.

'Please, Tom,' she said quietly.

'All right, Gaby,' he said at last, the smile fading. 'If that is what you want.' He disappeared back inside the house and Gaby sat on in the darkness.

Tom would tell Armand what she had said and he would read whatever interpretation into her message that he chose. A sudden breeze rippled round the courtyard, stirring the leaves of the eucalyptus tree— the tree she and Armand had sat beneath that day when he had come to see Oliver and caught her snoozing in the sun.

She mustn't think of that now, she thought desperately. But how could she help it? She loved him. How could she make that go away?

'Can I help at all, Gaby?' Tom was beside her again, his approach muffled by the soft shoes he was wearing.

She turned her head to look at him as he sat down beside her.

'You seem troubled,' he said.

'It's nothing, Tom.' She tried to keep her voice light, but was only too aware of the tremor in it. 'Really it isn't.'

'Fair enough.' He shrugged and was silent for a

moment, then he said quietly, 'But if there *was* something I would like to think you could share it with us, give us the opportunity of helping. You've been a tremendous help to Penny since you've been here—she's told me that—and we in turn would like to be there for you if you need us.'

'That is kind...' To her horror, Gaby felt her throat constrict and the tears well up in her eyes.

Tom must have been aware of her emotion because he carried on talking. 'Penny's been through a rough time lately,' he said. 'I've been pretty unbearable to live with—I know that. I was totally obsessed with the job and with getting on—you know, further and further up that career ladder. Well, to be honest with you, Gaby, I had put it before everything—Penny, the kids...'

'Your own health?' Gaby gulped, glad that the conversation had switched from her.

'Yes, even my own health,' he agreed. 'I had literally worked myself into the ground. I must have become totally impossible to live with...I don't know how Penny's put up with me. It's finally taken this business with the melanoma to show me what I stood to lose. Life is so precious, Gaby, and it isn't until it's threatened that we fully appreciate that fact.' He fell silent, and they both sat still in the darkness.

'Penny and I,' he went on after a while, 'have been doing a lot of talking in the last few days, and we've both agreed there are going to be some changes to our lifestyle. You simply can't go on burning the candle at both ends—because if you do, sooner or later, something's going to give.'

'I'm so glad you've realised that, Tom,' said Gaby quietly. 'I only wish my patients could see solutions so quickly.'

'It took a pretty drastic situation for me to come to accept it,' said Tom ruefully.

'Maybe...but at least you have accepted it, and you intend doing something about it.'

'So what about you?' Tom said after a moment. 'Will you be able to accept your particular situation?'

Gaby shrugged. 'It won't be easy,' she admitted at last.

'These things never are,' agreed Tom, then added, 'But, even more to the point, if you can accept it, will you be able to do anything about it?'

'Ah, now that would be a little more difficult.'

'Would I be permitted to ask why?' he said curiously, turning his head.

'Because,' she said, once more fighting her tears, 'it would involve my returning to England. To do that would be very hard, Tom, but I think, if I were to stay, it would break my heart.'

CHAPTER TWELVE

'GABY, what time is your first appointment?' Julie Roberts looked up from her desk.

'Ten-thirty,' replied Gaby, pausing on her way through the medical unit to her room. 'Why?' she added, noticing Julie's harassed expression.

'I was wondering if you could give me a hand for an hour or so.' Julie hesitated. 'I hate to ask, but Suzanne's going to be late and won't be in until about ten o'clock.'

'Yes, all right,' Gaby replied, but her heart sank. It had been her intention to shut herself away in her room that morning, so that she wouldn't have to see Armand, but if Julie wanted her help on the unit she would be bound to come into contact with him. 'I was only going to write up some reports,' she added. 'What would you like me to do?'

'It would be a great help if you could be here on Reception when the patients start to arrive. . .but before that, do you think you could help me put these supplies away?' Julie indicated a stack of cardboard packing cases that almost reached the ceiling.

'Sure.' Gaby moved round behind the desk to deposit her briefcase and jacket. When she turned it was to find Julie looking curiously at her.

'Are you all right?' she asked.

'Yes.' Gaby nodded and smoothed back her hair.

'You look very peaky this morning,' Julie went on doubtfully.

'Thanks, Julie.' Gaby gave a short laugh. 'Thanks a million. If I had been feeling under the weather that would have made me feel heaps better! But, no, I'm fine—really, I am. Just a bit tired, that's all—I didn't sleep very well last night.'

Gaby wondered what Julie would have thought if she'd known that she had, in fact, not slept at all the night before, that she had lain awake for hours listening for Oliver, agonising that she had inadvertently been responsible for creating the stress that could have caused his asthma attack, then battling with her own thoughts and emotions as they had chased each other round and round in her head.

She expected Julie to take herself off to the treatment room then, but instead she hovered, as if she wanted to say more but didn't quite know how. 'It's not Martin, is it, Gaby?' she said at last.

'What do you mean, Martin?' Gaby stared at her.

'Well, is it because of him that you're losing sleep?' asked Julie.

'Why should you think that?'

Julie looked embarrassed. 'I just wondered, that's all—how things were between you. . .'

'Martin Jackson and I are no longer an item,' said Gaby quietly. 'In fact, I doubt now that we ever were.'

'Oh, I see.' Julie stared at her, and for one moment Gaby thought that she detected relief on her face. 'So, did *you* end the relationship?' Julie went on after a moment.

'Yes, I did,' Gaby replied. 'I realised I was seeing Martin for all the wrong reasons—I certainly wasn't in love with him.'

'Well, that's a relief, I can tell you!' Julie let out her breath in a long sigh.

'I don't understand.' Gaby stared at her, wondering what on earth she could be talking about. 'Why should my finishing with Martin be a relief?'

'Well, it was last night, you see. . .' Julie hesitated again, then, as if coming to a rapid decision, she went on, 'I was out with Jean Paul. He took me to a restaurant down near the river, and while we were there Martin Jackson came in. . .he was with Suzanne. . .' She paused, glancing at Gaby to see what effect her words had. When Gaby remained silent she went on hurriedly, 'She had been like a cat on hot bricks all day yesterday, although she wouldn't say why. I can see now it was because he had asked her out. I fully intended asking her this morning what the hell was going on, then she phoned in to say she would be late...and you came in looking like death warmed up...'

'And you put two and two together and came up with five.' Gaby smiled. 'Don't worry, Julie, I can assure you my sleepless night had nothing whatsoever to do with Martin Jackson...or with Suzanne. If they are seeing each other, I say good luck to them.'

'Well, thank goodness for that.' Julie breathed a huge sigh of relief. 'I thought we were about to have all sorts of problems on the unit...' She trailed off and looked round. 'Well, this won't do. We'd better get stuck in to unpacking these supplies.'

They worked steadily for the next half-hour then, while Gaby was in the treatment room stacking crêpe bandages onto a shelf, she heard Armand's voice outside in Reception, and her knees suddenly felt as if they might be about to give way.

Cautiously she turned her head, and, looking over her shoulder, saw that he was talking to someone just outside her line of vision. She moved slightly, so that she could see who it was, then wished she hadn't. Armand and Mélisande had quite obviously arrived together and were talking quietly, their heads close. As she watched them, unobserved behind the shelter of the treatment room door, Gaby felt as if a knife had been thrust beneath her ribcage and that someone was twisting it.

Had Mélisande stayed at his house? Had they spent the night together? The secretary, as elegant and beautiful as ever, was wearing a black suit, the short skirt revealing her slim legs, while her dark hair, caught back at the nape of her neck, was fastened with a scarlet bow. Even as Gaby watched Mélisande, looking up into Armand's face, laughed at something he had just said.

The moment was intimate, private, and miserably Gaby turned back to what she was doing. Hélène's words echoed in her head—how these two had grown up together, been childhood sweethearts, how everyone knew that one day they would marry.

Why, oh why, had she allowed herself to fall in love with him? Anger welled up inside her—anger with herself for being so gullible. Helplessly she began moving the pile of crêpe bandages that she had just transferred from the carton to the shelf, taking them one by one and creating another pile only inches from the first.

'So there you are!' The voice was deep, the accent as sexily attractive as ever, as suddenly he was behind her.

Gaby froze, steeling herself for what might follow.

'I tried to phone you last night.'

She swallowed, afraid that her voice might have gone. 'Yes,' she said at last, without turning round, 'Tom said.'

'I wanted to apologise,' he went on, 'to you and to Oliver, for not seeing you both last evening.'

'It was nothing.' She gave a helpless little gesture with her hands. He was so close now that his face was touching her hair, and she could feel his breath, warm against her cheek.

'I think Oliver might have been disappointed. . .'

'He knows you are a busy man.' It sounded trite, even to herself, and Gaby sensed Armand's puzzlement as he drew slightly back.

'I was out,' he said. 'When I returned, Hélène said you and Oliver had gone.'

Out? She frowned. Did he intend lying to her now, on top of everything else? He had been in the house the previous evening. His car had been there. Mélisande's car had been there. She was certain that they had been together. . .in one of those shuttered rooms. . .

She began moving the bandages again, this time back to their original position.

Armand was silent for a moment, watching her, then uncertainly he said, 'You are helping Julie this morning?'

She nodded, then, as the futility of what she was doing finally hit her, she straightened up and took a deep breath. 'Yes,' she said crisply, 'and I must get on. I can hear patients arriving for surgery and I'm supposed to be on Reception.' Without allowing her gaze to meet his, she brushed past him and walked out of the treatment room, only too aware, however, of his air of bewilderment as he stood and watched her.

He was a good actor, she thought—feigning bewilderment, pretending not to understand her lack of response. But then he didn't know that she knew about Mélisande and himself, and even if he did he obviously assumed that it need make no difference to his relationship with her. Either he was oblivious to the way she felt about him, and his actions had simply been friendly concern, or—and somehow this prospect seemed even worse—he assumed that she would be available, even after he married Mélisande.

Somehow she got through the next half-hour on the reception desk. There seemed to be a great deal of activity between Julie and Mélisande, and much telephoning from Julie's office, but it was none of Gaby's business what it was about, and neither, the way she was feeling, did she really care. It was with a definite sense of relief, when Suzanne eventually arrived, that she was able to retreat at last to the sanctuary of her consulting room.

She saw two patients. One was the ongoing case of the young employee with alcohol-related problems, and the other was a new patient referred by Armand—a woman with relationship problems with her husband, brought about by unresolved childhood trauma.

The woman was in tears when she left the room, and as Gaby sat back in her chair and stretched her neck muscles to relieve some of her own tension her intercom sounded. With a sigh she flicked the switch.

'Gaby—' it was Suzanne's voice '—have you finished?'

'More or less.'

'Justin Metcalf has just come into Reception. He wants to see you.'

'You'd better send him along.'

'He doesn't have an appointment.'

'Never mind.'

'He says it won't take long. Oh—and Gaby?'

'Yes, Suzanne?' For one moment Gaby thought that Suzanne was going to say something about herself and Martin, but instead she said, 'When you've finished, Julie said could you come down to the unit? There's going to be a little celebration.'

'Sounds mysterious.'

'It is. None of us know what it's about.'

'OK. I'll be down—and tell Justin to come along.'

Moments later Justin knocked on her door, giving her no further opportunity to speculate. He looked sheepish, she thought as he came into the room and sat down.

'How are you, Justin?' She watched him closely, noting that he seemed more relaxed than on his previous visits.

'I'm OK.' He nodded. 'I just thought you might like to know I've decided to stay in Toulouse.'

'Really?' Gaby raised her eyebrows, but refrained from asking why.

'Yeah, well—' Justin shrugged '—they asked me if I wanted another contract here or whether I wanted to go home.'

'Last time we talked,' said Gaby slowly, 'I thought you said you were going home.'

'Yeah, well, I changed me mind, didn't I?' He hesitated, then said, 'I got thinking, you see.'

'What about, Justin?'

'Well. . .' He sighed. 'That accident. . .it got to me in a funny sort of way.'

'You mean the accident with the lorry?' For a moment Gaby wasn't sure whether he meant that or the accident of Claudine's pregnancy.

Justin nodded. 'I know accidents happen all the time,' he said, 'but, well, there's going to be an inquiry to find out who was responsible. . .right?'

'Yes.' Gaby nodded.

'Seems to me there's always someone responsible for everything. . .' He looked up sharply. 'Anyway,' he went on after a moment, 'it got me thinking. . . about something that you said, really. . .'

'Me?' Gaby raised her eyebrows.

'Yeah, when we were talking about Claudine and the baby you asked me what I was going t'do. You said it was my baby as much as hers. I'm responsible for that baby, aren't I, Mrs Dexter?'

'Yes, Justin,' she agreed quietly, then she added, 'You both are—you and Claudine.'

'I know, and it got me thinking. It's not really on for me to clear off back to England and just leave her to it.'

'So what do you intend doing?' Gaby was watching him closely again, and saw a tiny nerve flickering below one eye.

'I guess I'll stick around. At least 'til after the baby's born. After that, I'm not sure.' He shrugged. 'I'm not really into babies and all that stuff—and I'm not saying nothing about getting married either!'

'No, of course not.' Gaby suppressed a smile. 'Have you told Claudine about this yet?' she asked after a moment.

'Yeah,' Justin nodded. 'She was pleased. But I'm not promising nothing—not after the baby's born.'

'I think you are very wise, Justin,' Gaby said calmly. 'I think you should just take one day at a time.'

'It's like I said—' he looked pleased that Gaby seemed to be agreeing with him '—I don't know nothing about babies. . .and I bet it'll be a girl!'

'On the other hand, it could be a boy,' said Gaby seriously.

Justin paused, considering for a moment. 'Yeah. . .I suppose it could.' He grinned. The sullen expression disappeared, and as his face was suddenly transformed Gaby could see why the young French girl had been attracted to him. 'I could take it to see United play, couldn't I?' he added.

Gaby smiled. 'Fatherhood does have its compensations,' she said. 'But seriously, Justin, I'm glad you are going to stick around.'

He stood up. 'I have to go,' he said. 'Me next shift's just starting. . .but I just wanted you t'know. Oh, and I wanted to say thanks.'

Gaby smiled and walked to the door with him. 'I

didn't do much, Justin. You made the choice. I simply allowed you to talk through your options.'

'Yeah, well, whatever. See you, Mrs Dexter.'

She watched him stroll down the corridor, then she remembered Suzanne's message about a celebration. With a sigh she shut the door behind her, then she, too, began to walk towards the factory and the medical unit. A celebration was the last thing she felt like that day, but she knew that she must attempt to hide her feelings and join in. She didn't even know who the celebration was for, but she assumed that someone must be leaving and a presentation was about to be made.

There were a lot of people in the medical unit, standing about talking in small groups. Gaby caught a glimpse of Lisa Rayner through the crowd—a glowing Lisa, who was talking animatedly to one of the design engineers. There was champagne on Julie's desk, together with trays of glasses and plates of canapés.

Gaby allowed her gaze to wander round Reception. She had to find Armand. She didn't want to talk to him, but she needed to know where he was.

He was standing by the window, talking to a man whom Gaby had never seen before, a man with close-cropped hair, wearing small, wire-rimmed glasses.

As if he sensed her gaze on him, Armand looked up, and briefly their eyes met. Gaby felt as if her heart turned over, and when it looked as if Armand was trying to get away from his companion to join her she moved swiftly across the room, out of harm's way.

She began talking to one of the girls from Administration, a pleasant girl with short blonde hair who always wore huge earrings. In a kind of desperation Gaby focused her gaze onto the gold cones that dangled from the girl's ears, becoming almost mesmerised by their erratic movements until, sensing someone at her elbow, she turned abruptly and found Luc with a tray of champagne.

She took a glass, and was nibbling on a canapé that someone else had offered when the blonde girl suddenly said, 'Why is it she always manages to look fabulous?'

Gaby turned to see who she was talking about and saw Mélisande, on the far side of Reception, talking to Tom Shackleton who had just arrived. Gaby was about to ask the blonde girl if she knew who was leaving when Julie began to tap the side of her glass with a pen, to attract everyone's attention.

'As you will have gathered,' said Julie as a hush eventually descended, 'this is a very impromptu occasion. So impromptu, in fact, that even I knew nothing about it until this very morning. Nevertheless, it is an occasion that I'm sure you will all agree we couldn't let pass without celebrating. The fact that we are able to celebrate in style is thanks to Armand, who has provided the champagne.' She inclined her head towards Armand, and a ripple of laughter and applause ran round the room. 'And thanks to the ladies from Catering, who quickly rustled up some eats.' She paused and looked round, and again Gaby found herself wondering just who the celebration was for.

'The reason that I know you will all want to celebrate this occasion,' Julie went on after a moment, 'is because since she came to join us here at OBEX we have all become very fond of Mélisande. . .'

Mélisande? Gaby, aware of Armand's eyes on her once more, had been gazing into her glass. Now, sharply, she looked up. Was Mélisande leaving?

'We have all at some time,' Julie was continuing, 'been guests at Mélisande's home and enjoyed her particular brand of hospitality.' She paused, smiling at Mélisande, who tilted her head slightly in response. Then, as people nodded and murmured, there was another spontaneous ripple of applause.

'And now,' Julie went on, 'now that she is getting engaged, I know you will all want to join me in wishing her and her fiancé all the happiness in the world.'

Gaby drew in her breath so sharply that a crumb from the canapé she was nibbling caught in her throat.

Mélisande getting engaged? Mélisande and Armand? Was that what this was all about?

Wildly she looked around, and the sea of smiling faces seemed to lurch sickeningly towards her. Then, as the crumb in her throat began to tickle, she started to cough. With tears streaming down her cheeks, she turned and began to push her way blindly through the crowd.

'I say, are you all right, Gaby?' someone said.

'Have a drink of water,' the blonde girl called, her earrings bouncing furiously.

'Champagne would do.'

Someone thrust a glass towards her, but she brushed it aside and bolted for the door. Coughing or no coughing, she had to get out. Couldn't bear to stay there. To stay and see the pair of them. To have to congratulate them when she felt as if she'd just been torn apart.

She ran out of the unit and took a short cut through the factory, through the noise—the hammering and drilling, the whistling and shouting of the men high above on the jigs—then outside into the hot, midday sun as for the second time in two days Gaby found herself making a hasty retreat, and for more or less the same reasons.

Hurrying to her car, she unlocked it, slipped inside and, wiping her eyes with the back of her hand, she started the engine then drove away. Suddenly the most important thing in the world was to get away from the factory, from Julie and the others and their celebrations, and from Mélisande's smiling face.

But most important of all she had to get away from Armand, who, whether she was prepared to admit it or not, still had the power to hurt her.

There was no recital that afternoon, neither was anyone rehearsing, so the peace in the coolness of the cloisters was absolute.

Gaby sat on a low wall, her back against one of the stone columns, and watched a small lizard as it darted back and forth on the flagstones in the sun-drenched courtyard.

She wasn't sure why she had come to the Jacobin; she only knew that she'd had to get away from the factory and what was being celebrated. She hadn't wanted to go back to the house, because Penny or Adèle would have been bound to ask awkward questions at her appearance in the middle of the day. Besides, she had to stay in Toulouse, she had to go back to work later—she had patients to see. She could phone and say she was sick, but it wouldn't be true, and she had an obligation to her patients.

Hopefully, by then, Armand would have gone.

The lizard suddenly darted up the wall and paused in front of her, then, realising that it was in the shadow cast by the stone column, scuttled back to the sunlight where it lay motionless, its tiny limbs splayed on the flagstone.

How could Armand have done it? She swallowed, watching the lizard with brimming, unseeing eyes. How could he have kissed her the way he had, led her to believe that he cared for her, when all the time he'd been planning his engagement to Mélisande? It seemed more than likely now that what Hélène had said was right, that he'd planned to marry Mélisande but carry on seeing her as well.

A surge of anger flared inside her at the thought, and she curled her hands into tight fists.

'Gabrielle.' The voice, coming from the depths of the cloisters, was low and instantly recognisable, but even if it hadn't been she would have known it was him because he was the only one who called her Gabrielle. But how had he known where to find her? She looked up sharply and saw him walking towards her out of the shadows.

Wildly she looked around, but this time there was no escape. The only way out appeared to be through the one entrance, and if she made for that it would mean passing him.

His footsteps grew closer, ringing out on the flagstones. Then he was standing before her, looking down at her. Helplessly she turned her face away.

Irrelevantly she realised that the lizard had fled, darting away into the base of one of the tall, thin conifers that dotted the courtyard. Gaby wished that she could do the same.

'I guessed you were here,' he said quietly. 'I followed you for a while, then I lost you in the traffic. I thought you might have gone back to St Michel, but something told me to look here first. I saw your car outside.'

He had answered her question as to how he had found her; now she wondered why he had followed her. Surely he should be back there with Mélisande, celebrating their engagement. Before she could speak he sat down on the wall facing her.

'What is it, Gabrielle?' he said at last. 'What is wrong?'

'How can you even ask that?' She couldn't bring herself to look at him, but her voice sounded strained even to herself, and Armand could not have failed to detect her pent up anger.

'I don't understand,' he said, and when at last she looked up she saw that there was a puzzled frown on his face. 'You appeared to choke,' he went on, 'then you ran from the unit. At first I thought you might be ill—that was why I followed you—then from the window I saw you getting into your car. I became really alarmed then. . . What is it Gabrielle?' He leaned forward. 'Please tell me.' He reached out and touched her hands, would have taken them in his, but she snatched them away.

'Gabrielle!'

She was aware of the bewilderment and the pain in his eyes but she was glad, because suddenly she wanted to hurt him—to hurt him as much as he had hurt her.

'I don't understand what has happened to you,' he said after a moment. 'The other evening when I came out to St Michel everything seemed so good between us. I thought. . .' Helplessly he spread his hands, and Gaby found herself thinking once again what a superb actor he was.

Then, quite suddenly, his eyes narrowed. 'Is this anything to do with Monsieur Jackson?' he asked quietly. 'Has he been pressurising you again?'

She shook her head. 'No,' she said tightly. 'Martin's got nothing to do with it.'

'Then what?'

She remained silent, while nearby a bell began to toll.

'I can't think,' said Armand, 'what could have happened to bring about this change in you.'

As the last notes of the bell died away, leaving only the echo in the cloisters, Gaby said tightly, 'Maybe you should try asking Hélène.'

'Hélène?' Armand looked up sharply. 'What does Hélène have to do with anything?'

Gaby gave a slight shrug, and turned away from him.

He remained silent for a long moment, then he said curiously, 'When you came to my house yesterday, did you and Hélène talk?'

'Of course we did. I had a lesson.'

'Apart from your lesson.'

'We may have done.' She gave a light shrug.

'Gabrielle, please. . .' A note of exasperation had crept into his voice. 'What did Hélène tell you? I must know.'

When still she said nothing, he gave a sigh. 'I think I can guess,' he said.

Gaby raised her eyebrows.

'Correct me if I'm wrong,' said Armand, and his tone was both knowing, yet somehow sceptical, 'but I would say that she told you something about Mélisande Legrande—am I right?'

'She told me Mélisande was her niece,' said Gaby. 'I had no idea of that. It would have been nice if I had known.'

'I never thought to tell you,' Armand said slowly, 'I didn't consider it important.'

She looked up sharply and a shaft of sunlight filtered through the stone columns, catching her hair and turning it to burnished copper. 'Just as you never thought it important to tell me anything else about Mélisande Legrande?' She could feel her anger beginning to rise again as she remembered how he had conned her into believing that she was special to him, when all the time. . .all the time he was planning to. . .

'What else did Hélène tell you?' he asked urgently, breaking in on her thoughts.

Gaby didn't answer immediately, searching for the right words. 'She told me about two children playing together in the vineyards,' she said at last, the words tumbling out, as if in some way she could release her pain along with them. 'Two children who became childhood sweethearts,' she rushed on. 'She told me of those children growing up, of a pact between them, of an understanding between two families that those same children one day would marry.' She was aware of the bitterness that had crept into her voice, but she did nothing to disguise it.

'That sort of thing happens frequently between families,' said Armand. 'Especially where there are friendships, businesses, land and properties. But when children grow up they realise that what happened between them need not necessarily still be right.'

'Only in this case it *was* right, wasn't it, Armand?' Angrily Gaby stood up and stared down at him. 'The family agreement between you and Mélisande quite obviously survived the intervening years, just as the personal one did—today has been proof of that. But why did you lead me to believe there was also something special between us?' Her eyes filled with hot, angry tears, and she became aware that Armand had also risen to his feet.

Then, as the tears began to overflow and course down her cheeks, he stepped towards her.

'Damn you, Armand!' she cried, and the profanity seemed even more pronounced within the sanctity of the monastery walls. Raising her clenched hands, she began to beat ineffectually against his chest. 'I suppose you thought you could marry Mélisande,' she choked, 'and keep me as your mistress, tucked away somewhere, to use whenever you felt like it. . .'

'Gabrielle. . .' He caught her wrists but she swept on, determined to allow nothing to stop what she had to say.

'You criticised Martin when you thought he only

wanted to live with me and not marry me, but what you were planning, Armand Laurent, was a hundred times worse!' She gasped for breath. 'Maybe to you this sort of thing is an everyday occurrence, but I can tell you now, we don't behave like that where I come from! Oh!' She gasped again as suddenly Armand pulled her roughly into his arms.

'Let me go!' she cried. 'How dare you? You have no right to do that—!' She was silenced by his mouth covering hers, his hard, lean body pressing hers against the stone column.

She couldn't let this happen. This was the last thing she wanted now. She had only just managed to resist him, to tell him what she thought of him, to keep him at arm's length, to be angry with him.

But now, with his arms around her, his body against hers, his tongue parting her lips, what chance would she have?

Her treacherous body began its inevitable betrayal, and as the demands of his hands and lips grew ever more urgent Gaby felt her resistance begin to ebb slowly away.

'Gabrielle, Gabrielle.' He whispered her name over and over again, the whispers echoing throughout the cloisters until finally she gave up the battle and surrendered.

Her arms crept around his neck, her fingers sank into his hair, and her breasts strained against the thin cotton fabric of her blouse as, deep inside, she once again felt the stirrings of desire. Her anger turned to yearning, and her need for him grew to a wanting that threatened to overwhelm them both.

For one moment, in the madness of the noonday sun, she thought he would take her there and then, make love to her on the cool flagstones.

Then, abruptly, as if they both became aware of where they were, they drew apart, panting, eyeing each other, shocked at the intensity of their feelings and at what had so nearly happened.

Gaby spoke first, her voice little more than a whispered sob. 'Go away, Armand,' she said. 'Get out of my life. Go to Mélisande and keep your promise to her!'

'Gabrielle—' Almost brutally he jerked her to him again, his fingers tightly gripping her upper arms. 'I have no intention of marrying Mélisande!'

'What?' Wildly she stared at him. He was hurting her, but she ignored it. 'How can you to stand there and say that?' she demanded.

'Because it is the truth.'

'But...but... Hélène said...'

'Forget what Hélène said. She is clinging to old ideals, old dreams.'

'But...the celebration...you can't deny that...I was there, Armand,' she cried. 'I saw...I heard.'

'You saw what, Gabrielle? Heard what?' His grip tightened and she flinched.

'Mélisande... Julie said she was to be married...'

'And because of what Hélène had told you, you assumed it was me she was marrying?'

'Yes...' She stared at him, wide-eyed.

'Gabrielle...' With a sigh he released her arms. Then gently he put his hands on her shoulders and guided her back to the low wall, forcing her to sit down again. 'You listened to Hélène,' he said, sitting close beside her, 'now will you listen to me?'

'But...'

'Please, Gabrielle.'

'All right.' She nodded, wondering whatever she could be about to hear.

'What Hélène told you was right,' he said. 'At least, to a point it was. Mélisande is her niece. When she was a child, her mother used to work at Château Laurent. Our families were close friends.' He nodded, then paused, as if choosing his words with great care, while Gaby waited in an agony of suspense.

'Mélisande and I grew up together,' he continued at last, 'and, yes, it was assumed that one day we would marry.'

Gaby felt the breath catch in her throat, but before she could say anything Armand went on speaking.

'We were close, very close—still are, for that matter,' he admitted. 'But the love I feel for Mélisande is more the love a brother may feel for his sister—'

'In that case,' Gaby cried passionately, interrupting him, 'how can you even think of—?'

'Please, Gabrielle,' Armand said, 'let me finish.' When she fell silent again, he went on, 'During the passing of time I felt that Mélisande's feelings for me had also changed. She came to my home frequently—sometimes as my guest, sometimes to visit Hélène, her aunt, whom I had employed when she lost her job as a teacher. I did nothing about clarifying my relationship with Mélisande because the need never arose. The situation suited us both. . .'

He paused again, reflecting, and Gaby found herself recalling that first time she had been to his house. She had heard a woman's laughter, caught the scent of her perfume. Mélisande had been there then. Now, from what Armand was telling her, it seemed that it was the most natural thing in the world that she should have been there.

'We went out together sometimes. . .' He shrugged. 'We remained close. Then, Gabrielle, I met you—and suddenly, in a very short space of time, everything changed. You turned my world upside down with your fiery hair, your lovely smile. I could not get you out of my thoughts. You were there, haunting me at every moment of the day and of the night. Soon I realise I am in love with you.' He picked up her hand, uncurled her fingers and implanted a kiss on the palm, then folded her fingers again over the spot, as if to keep it safe.

'Armand. . .' She could only whisper, for her heart had begun to beat very fast and she could not trust her voice.

'Wait.' He held up his hand, gently silencing her again. 'I decided,' he went on, 'that I needed to see Mélisande and explain to her, in the hopes that she would understand. I was, you see, only too aware of the old ties and loyalties that still seemed to bind us together, but I was not sure how Mélisande felt. I did not want to hurt her. . .'

'So what happened? Did she understand?' Gaby frowned, not sure now that even she understood what was happening.

'It was even better than that.' Armand smiled suddenly, and Gaby found herself watching him closely, loving every expression, every gesture—the way his lips curved, the way the skin at the corners of his eyes crinkled when he smiled.

'I asked Mélisande to come to my house late yesterday afternoon,' he went on after a moment. 'Hélène was there, so I suggested we went out to a café where we could talk. I told her about you, Gabrielle, and what I felt was happening between us. I was apprehensive as to what her reaction would be, so, as you can imagine, I was relieved when she told me how pleased she was for me. She said she liked you, and had instinctively felt we would be right for each other. She had even suspected we might be attracted to one another.'

'She said that?' Gaby stared at him.

'Yes, but that was not all.' Armand paused, a smile on his lips. 'I could hardly believe it when she went on to tell me that she too had fallen in love with someone else. He is a lawyer, and lives and works in Paris—she met him only recently at a party. He had asked her to marry him and she had been. . .how you say?. . .plucking up? Is that right?'

Gaby nodded weakly.

'Plucking up the courage,' he went on, 'to tell me. You see, Mélisande also knew the feeling between us could never be right for marriage, but she wasn't certain how I felt.'

'But. . .today. . .what was all that about?' Gaby gazed at him, still bewildered, even though the mists in her mind were gradually beginning to lift. 'I thought the celebration was for Mélisande. . .?'

'It was. . .but for Mélisande and her lawyer.' Armand smiled. 'After she left me last night she phoned Philippe in Paris and told him she would marry him. He flew down to Toulouse this morning. When he arrived at OBEX Julie decided it called for a celebration. Apparently she had known Mélisande's secret from the start...'

'So he was there today... Mélisande's lawyer?' Gaby's eyes widened in amazement.'

'Yes—I had a brief talk with him. I got the impression he was nervous of meeting me...'

Gaby suddenly recalled the man she'd seen talking to Armand, and instinctively knew that that had been Philippe.

'He seemed nice,' Armand went on. 'I only hope he makes Mélisande happy...' He trailed off and allowed his gaze to wander over Gaby. 'You thought that celebration was for Mélisande and me, didn't you?' he asked softly. When she nodded, he sighed. '*Ah, ma pauvre petite*...' Lapsing into French, he put his arm round her, drawing her close.

'I wish someone had told me,' she whispered, burying her face against his shirt.

'I tried to,' he murmured. 'Last evening, when Mélisande and I got back to the house, you and Oliver had gone, so I tried to phone you. Tom said you weren't available. Then this morning I tried to talk to you, but you would not listen to me...I thought I had upset you in some way.'

'Oh, Armand,' she whispered.

They remained together in silence for a while, his arm around her, her head against his chest, then she broke the silence.

'Does Hélène know any of this?' she asked curiously.

He nodded. 'Yes, when we got back to the house Mélisande told her that Philippe had asked her to marry him.'

'What was her reaction?'

'She was upset,' he admitted. 'But...' he paused '...she said nothing about her conversation with you.'

'She doesn't like me,' said Gaby. 'She didn't like me from the start. She only agreed to give me lessons because you asked her to and she probably didn't dare refuse.'

'I am not sure it was you she did not like,' Armand said thoughtfully, 'rather the situation. Hélène must have seen the way it was between us right from the start—she saw you as a threat to Mélisande. Now you are no longer a threat, it will be different.'

'What about your mother?'

Armand smiled. 'What does my mother have to do with it?'

'According to Hélène, your mother was as set on you and Mélisande marrying as she was.'

'She may have been once,' he agreed, 'but my mother is a realist—it's what makes her a good businesswoman. Besides, when she meets you she will know why I have to marry you.' Leaning forward, he kissed the tip of her nose.

'And while we are on that subject,' he went on after a moment, 'I think our visit to Château Laurent is well overdue.'

While Gaby's brain was still trying to cope with all he had said he went on, 'I suggest we go this weekend. But first there are two other matters that need attention.'

'There are?' she murmured, dazed by the pace of what was happening.

He nodded. 'We must talk to Oliver.'

'Oliver?'

'Yes. I think Oliver should be the first to be told what is happening,' said Armand quietly. 'After all, he may not approve. He did not seem too pleased with Martin Jackson. Who knows? He may feel the same way about me.'

'I can assure you, you need have no fears on that score.' Gaby smiled and shook her head, then, as the full force of all he had said finally hit her, she took a deep breath and threw Armand a quick glance, 'You said two things needed attention?'

'Yes,' he agreed, 'I did.'

'So what is the other?'

'The other,' he said, his gaze wandering over her face, lingering on her mouth and finally coming to rest on her eyes, 'needs to be attended to even before we go to see Oliver.'

'Oh, why is that?' She in turn allowed her gaze to

roam over his features, focusing at last on the sensual curve of his lips while at the same time longing for him to kiss her again.

'Because,' he said softly, his accent becoming even more pronounced, 'it is no good going to Oliver until I have the answer I want.' He stood up and moved round in front of her, then, taking her hands in his, he drew her to her feet. 'Gabrielle,' he said, his voice grown suddenly husky, 'you will marry me, won't you?'

She stared into his eyes, thinking that she could quite happily drown in their depths, then, as she realised what he had said, an overwhelming feeling of love and certainty flooded her heart.

'Please, Gabrielle,' he entreated, 'say you will.'

'Oh, Armand,' she whispered, 'of course I will.'

In the moment that his lips touched hers the bell began to toll for a second time, adding its own approval as they sealed their intention with a kiss.

Delicious Dishes

Would you like to win a year's supply of simply irresistible romances? Well, you can and they're FREE! Simply match the dish to its country of origin and send your answers to us by 31st December 1996. The first 5 correct entries picked after the closing date will win a year's supply of Temptation novels (four books every month—worth over £100). What could be easier?

A	LASAGNE		GERMANY
B	KORMA		GREECE
C	SUSHI		FRANCE
D	BACLAVA		ENGLAND
E	PAELLA		MEXICO
F	HAGGIS		INDIA
G	SHEPHERD'S PIE		SPAIN
H	COQ AU VIN		SCOTLAND
I	SAUERKRAUT		JAPAN
J	TACOS		ITALY

Please turn over for details of how to enter 👉

How to enter

Listed in the left hand column overleaf are the names of ten delicious dishes and in the right hand column the country of origin of each dish. All you have to do is match each dish to the correct country and place the corresponding letter in the box provided.

When you have matched all the dishes to the countries, don't forget to fill in your name and address in the space provided and pop this page into an envelope (you don't need a stamp) and post it today! Hurry—competition ends 31st December 1996.

**Mills & Boon Delicious Dishes
FREEPOST
Croydon
Surrey
CR9 3WZ**

Are you a Reader Service Subscriber? Yes ❏   No ❏

Ms/Mrs/Miss/Mr _____

Address _____

_____

_____ Postcode _____

One application per household.

You may be mailed with other offers from other reputable companies as a result of this application. If you would prefer not to receive such offers, please tick box. ❏

C396
F